Wishing you

hours with your grandchildren,

Alexander James.
26th May 2010.

Dragon Riders

ALEXANDER LAWES

authorHOUSE®

AuthorHouse™
1663 Liberty Drive
Bloomington, IN 47403
www.authorhouse.com
Phone: 1-800-839-8640

This book is a work of fiction. People, places, events, and situations are the product of the author's imagination. Any resemblance to actual persons, living or dead, or historical events, is purely coincidental.

© 2010 Alexander Lawes. All rights reserved.

No part of this book may be reproduced, stored in a retrieval system, or transmitted by any means without the written permission of the author.

First published by AuthorHouse 2/17/2010

ISBN: 978-1-4490-8583-4 (sc)

Printed in the United States of America
Bloomington, Indiana

This book is printed on acid-free paper.

For my wife and children

Grateful acknowledgement is made to
Darin Jewel of The Inspira Group

Chapter 1

Brothers

Snow had fallen thickly all night long, and now in the early hours of morning, it lay deeply, blanketing the countryside. It was still dark as three small shadowy figures slipped through the back door of the old monastery. Carefully, they closed the heavy oak door behind them and turned the key in the lock. Two boys and a girl shivered against the cold air, and pulled their cloaks tightly about their bodies. The extra layers that they were wearing did little to keep out the bitter easterly wind. Their clothes were not the type to protect against extreme weather. One of the boys stomped his boots heavily to keep warm.

"Shush," hissed his two companions.

"Do you want us to get caught before we've even had a chance to try out this?" said Daniel. He was holding a large wooden sledge, which he shook vigorously in front of the other boy's face.

"I'm sorry," said Joe, shivering. "It's just that I've never felt so cold."

"Come on, let's go," hissed Liselle at the boys, "or are you two going to stand around gossiping like a couple of old fish-wives?"

Before they could answer, she turned away, smirking as she did so, and trotted silently across the garden towards the iron gate in the far wall. The boys followed quickly behind her, the snow crunching underfoot. The gate creaked noisily as Liselle swung it open, and sounded to them as if it might awaken the entire country. They held their breaths, expecting uproar from within the monastery, but all remained quiet. Swiftly they slipped through the gateway, and skirting the old building, they kept low behind the outer wall before heading off into the fields. They stayed close to the hedges, keeping out of sight of any watchful eyes. Liselle and Joe ran ahead and Daniel followed, pulling the sledge behind him.

"What if someone sees our tracks?" asked Joe, when he and Liselle stopped for a rest some way from the monastery.

"They will see our tracks, we know that. Look, we know we're going to get caught eventually, but it'll be worth it," replied Liselle. "Now come on, will you, before the monks wake up and realise that we're missing."

"Yes, come on Daniel, please try to keep up," said Joe.

Daniel had been lagging behind and had just caught up with Liselle and Joe. He gasped breathlessly at Joe's remark, but before he had had time to complain or even to rest, they were off again into the dark.

It was the first time that any of them had ever seen snow and they intended to make the most of it, despite the inevitable consequences. Daniel took a deep breath, and lowering his head, he pulled hard on the rope and trudged through the thick snow after his friends.

After a lot of puffing and panting, they reached the top of the hill that overlooked the monastery and looked about them. The snow stretched across the countryside to every horizon. They stood and watched as the sun rose, turning the snow covered landscape a pale red.

"It looks like blood," stated Daniel.

"No, blood's much darker than that," said Joe.

"Oh, and since when did you become the world's authority on the colour of blood?" teased Daniel.

"Since last year, when I fell down the stairs and smacked my nose on the floor," replied Joe knowledgably.

"Good point," said Liselle. "I'd almost forgotten about that. I didn't think you were ever going to stop bleeding."

"I should have remembered," added Daniel. "I was the one who had to clear it all up."

"Well then you shouldn't have tripped me in the first place, should you?"

"It was an accident, alright?"

"So you keep saying, but we've only got your word for it," said Joe, grinning at his friend.

They looked back the way they had come. Half a mile away to the south, they could see the monastery and a little way beyond lay the snow-capped village of Crickle. Small villages with their prominent churches dotted the white landscape. Well-kept farms were surrounded by neat little fields and on the horizon lay the nearest town.

"How far is it to Southersby?" asked Joe, looking towards the town.

"About twenty miles by road I think," answered Liselle. "I remember passing through it on my way here," she added quietly, thinking back to that painful day.

The three friends gazed awkwardly in silence, each remembering their own arrival at the monastery.

"The old place doesn't look so big from up here," said Daniel, breaking the uneasy quiet. "I thought the place was huge on my first day."

They never referred to it as the orphanage, choosing rather to say the monastery, as though it was easier to cope.

The orphanage was once a monastery. When the war came, its function changed to accommodate some of the many children made homeless by the fighting. The monks had offered to stay on and look after the orphans. It was their contribution to the war, since they were not prepared to fight. Most of the children had lost one or even both parents, while a few were unfortunate enough to have lost their entire families. Everybody was affected by the war to some degree.

Daniel had lost his parents when he was very young, so had never known them. They had lived near the border and died defending their home during one of the first raids. A neighbour had managed to smuggle the infant out of the town and delivered him to a relative. Thereafter he had been passed around by his relatives, none of them particularly wanting him. At the age of seven, he was finally carted off to the orphanage by someone who called herself his dear aunt, but had been anything but. The last five years had actually been the happiest he had ever known. Although the monks were strict, he at least had felt part of a family and had made easy friends of the other children at the orphanage.

Joe had arrived shortly after Daniel and they became fast friends. Joe's mother, at least, was alive and well, and worked as a nurse for the army. He wrote to her often and she visited him three or four times a year. Joe's father had been captured at about the same time that Daniel's parents had been killed, but no one knew what had happened to him.

Like Daniel, Liselle's parents had both been killed, and she and her older brother had been sent to the orphanage. Unlike Daniel however, Liselle remembered her parents all too well. They had died in an accident when she was eight.

Liselle looked down at the sledge. It had belonged to her brother Charlie. She hadn't seen him now for over a year. Charlie had run away from the orphanage to join the army. Not being very academically minded, he saw no reason to stay until he was sixteen, as was expected. His daring escape made him an instant legend in the eyes of the remaining children. The stories were incredible, but Liselle alone knew the truth. She had never revealed it to anybody until the snow had arrived a week ago.

Not long after Charlie's departure Liselle received a letter from him, which was handed over by the monks somewhat begrudgingly. Swiftly, he had made contact with an army recruitment centre. There were plenty around so it hadn't taken him long. He was only fifteen, but since he looked older, lying about his age was easy so they had taken him on. Army life suited Charlie. He liked things to be nice and orderly. The routine that the monks imposed at the orphanage had conditioned him in this respect.

Woodwork had been his only interest at the orphanage. Of all things, he had built a sledge, during one particularly long summer. The other monks disapproved, but the kindly monk who took the woodworking class pointed out that there was no harm, since it had not snowed for over fifty years. Quite where Charlie had found inspiration for the design of the sledge nobody knew, but the finished product was a masterpiece. Even the abbot admitted that he had rarely seen such craftsmanship, and the sledge was duly put on display in the main hall, where it had resided ever since.

Charlie had made one other thing in secret. It was a large wooden key, an exact copy of the iron key for the kitchen door that led into the kitchen gardens, and he had used it to leave the monastery one dark night. He spoke to Liselle from outside one of the open windows of her dormitory.

"Promise me one thing. If it snows, use the sledge," he whispered. "Here, you'll need the key to get out."

He passed the wooden replica through the bars to Liselle. The bars were there to protect the children, the monks said. The bars also did a good job of keeping them in. There was probably some truth in the monks' explanation, as they were, after all, in the middle of a war with Koronia.

"Keep the key hidden. Don't tell anyone about it, not even your two friends."

Charlie winked at his little sister.

"But I wouldn't want to risk breaking the sledge," argued Liselle.

"It doesn't matter," whispered Charlie. "You'll probably only have one shot anyway before the monks catch up with you. All I ask is that you tell me the whole story next time we meet."

Liselle nodded, struggling to keep down the lump swelling in her throat.

"Of course, it'll probably never snow anyway," said Charlie sadly.

She reached back through the bars to her brother. Giving her hand a firm squeeze, Charlie gave his sister one last smile and disappeared into the night.

Liselle had never felt so alone. Even when her parents had died, Charlie had always been there for her. She knew that she still had her friends, but until now, she was one of the lucky ones that had family close by. With Charlie gone, she was no different to the other orphans.

That had been over a year ago. Charlie had written regularly, and Liselle eventually got used to him not being around. The thought of also losing her brother terrified her, but his frequent letters let her know that all was well.

The monks, although pleasant enough, would not tolerate any kind of games or playing, so there was no chance that they would allow any use of the sledge. It was a strict policy of working and learning that they ran at the orphanage.

There was however one monk in particular whom they all liked. His name was Brother Bartholomew but he preferred to be called Bart. He was always kind and always helpful, and he was never cruel to any of them. An orphan himself, he could remember what it had been like to be young and parentless, and so he sympathised with them. He also happened to teach woodwork.

There was only one area of magic that the monks would teach them, which was Protective Charms. The monks would never teach anything deemed aggressive or violent, so that left only self-defence. Protective Charms was about the only magic that could be done without the use of a Power Bracelet. For all the monk's talk about peace and self defence, the abbot and a couple of the more senior monks did wear Bracelets; for the safety of the monastery, of course.

Joe struggled to concentrate in most lessons and never did very well in tests, but in Protective Charms, he excelled. He was particularly good at the Repulsing Charm due, according to the abbot, to Joe being a repulsive little boy. The abbot, who taught Protective Charms, always laughed at his own jokes, but the class refused to join in. Joe was well liked and the pupils would much rather watch the abbot squirm when nobody laughed with him. Trying to repress their laughter was usually funnier than the jokes, so often they would end up laughing anyway. The abbot would beam delightedly on these occasions, naively unaware of the reality of the situation.

The monks deemed the orphan's use of charms on one another far too dangerous. When they practised the Repulsing Charm, they would be paired off and each given a small inoffensive ball. One would roll the ball, very slowly of course, towards their partner. The receiver would concentrate his or her mind and utter the charm. With a bit of practise and considerable luck, the ball would rebound back away. If they were sufficiently adept, the ball would bounce back and forth between them.

Joe was so proficient, he had discovered that if he willed hard enough, rather than using the charm to repulse, he could use it to move an already stationary object. He kept this knowledge to himself, but on one occasion, struggling to hold back, he caused the ball to fly through the air and smash through one of the stained glass windows. The abbot accused Joe of kicking the ball, and Daniel and Liselle defended him instantly, having seen for themselves what Joe had just done. Joe however, unusually sensibly for him, admitted to the abbot that he had indeed kicked the ball, and was willing to accept whatever punishment the abbot deemed necessary. Daniel and Liselle could only stand, open mouthed, unable to believe what they were hearing. The abbot was so surprised by Joe's supposed honesty that he forgot to punish him for the smashed window, and in confusion, he sent Joe's friends to clear up the broken glass.

When they met up again at lunchtime, Joe apologised and explained, "This is something I don't want the monks to know about. I've been practising a lot recently and suspected that I might be capable of much more. Now that I know, I want to keep it quiet."

What Joe said did make sense. If the abbot got wind of Joe's ability, he would probably stop Joe from attending Protective Charms. His skill would be seen as a potentially offensive capability that could be used as a weapon.

They learned other charms such as Healing, which they could only really practise when they injured themselves. This was rare, since they were allowed to do very little that could cause harm.

Levitation was completely pointless. No one had ever witnessed it for real, and most of them suspected it to be a ruse to keep them quiet, whilst they concentrated on the impossible. Quite how this could be used to protect oneself when assaulted was anybody's guess.

Invisibility was another bogus charm. Lying prostrate on the ground with one's eyes squeezed tightly shut didn't seem to make any of them disappear. The best anyone could hope for was that the attacker might think that you were dead already.

Translation was an especially clever charm that enabled the listener to understand a foreign tongue. Only it had no use in a land where everybody spoke the same language.

Overall, life at the monastery wasn't too bad, but it did lack one thing, and that was excitement.

"Bye then," called Liselle from behind the boys. She was running towards the far side of the hill and pushing the sledge in front of her.

"Quick, she's going without us," shouted Joe, rushing to catch up.

Liselle jumped forwards onto the sledge, sliding herself up to the front. She stretched her legs onto the runners that curved up gracefully and held the rope tightly. Joe caught Liselle quickly and jumped on behind her, giving the sledge an extra burst of speed. Daniel was a little slower than the others but eventually managed to catch up and leapt onto the back of the runners, where he stood behind Joe, holding onto his friend's shoulders. As they approached the edge, he gave one last push with his foot and they shot down the slope.

Gathering speed rapidly, they shrieked with exhilaration as the sledge careered down the steep hillside. Liselle attempted to steer with little success, preferring to yell out commands to lean one way or the other, which the boys did their very best to ignore so that their descent was completely out of control. This, of course, meant that their ride was all the more riotous.

At the bottom of the hill, the sledge and its three passengers glided to a graceful halt.

"Your brother's a genius," exclaimed Daniel, jumping off the back and sinking into the soft snow.

Joe agreed readily, "The next time I see him I'm telling him just that."

Liselle smiled appreciatively and picked up the rope. "Up the next hill then?" she asked, gesturing towards the much larger hill in front of them.

Daniel led the way up, cutting a path though the deep snow. Liselle pulled on the rope and Joe pushed the sledge from behind. Despite the bitterly cold wind, by the time they crested the next hilltop all three were sweating. As they regained their breath and viewed the next descent, they cooled rapidly.

"Let's not hang about then," said Joe rubbing his hands together to keep warm.

Liselle and Daniel didn't need telling twice and jumped onto the sledge, causing it to sink into the snow.

"I'll just get on the back then shall I?" asked Joe sarcastically.

"If you like," answered Daniel looking straight ahead and trying not to laugh.

"Come on Joe, give us a push," said Liselle.

Joe tried to push the sledge but it was stuck.

"It's too flat here," observed Daniel. "We'll have to push it over to the edge."

"Why bother?" asked Liselle, turning around. "Joe can push us from here, can't you," she said looking up at him.

Daniel laughed but stopped short when he saw that Liselle was serious. Joe's own indignation faded, as he understood Liselle's meaning.

"Okay, I'll give it a go," he said hesitantly and closed his eyes. Joe relaxed his mind and focused on the sledge. Then he whispered the Repulsing Charm and with a slight jolt, they were propelled along at a leisurely pace. Joe opened his eyes but continued to concentrate, keeping the power of the charm active. The sledge moved across the top of the hill, accelerating slowly as gradually the front of the sledge rose up out of the slow until they were skimming once more across the top of the white powder.

Then they pitched fiercely over the ridge that surrounded the hilltop and sped down the steep side. They accelerated rapidly and hung on desperately. Suddenly a large tree appeared directly in their way.

"Lean over to the left," yelled Liselle, pulling fiercely on the rope.

They lurched to one side, narrowly avoiding the tree as the sledge lifted up on one runner. As the sledge righted itself again, too late they saw the next obstacle in their path. It was a small hillock, which they crested at top speed, sailing effortlessly into the empty air.

They crashed in a sprawling heap, laughing and shouting at each other, the thick soft snow cushioning their fall.

"If I'd known you two were going to be so useless, I would have left you behind and come by myself," said Liselle pompously, with a twinkle in her eye.

The boys glanced at Liselle and then looked at each other, and then they burst into laughter, throwing snowballs at one another.

"Since when did you ever do anything by yourself?" accused Joe.

"Since when did any of us do anything by ourselves?" added Daniel.

"One tree on the whole hillside and you had to aim straight for it!" accused Joe between fits of laughter.

"Maybe we should have tried the other left?" suggested Liselle.

"Right?" said Joe, a little bemused.

"Exactly," agreed Daniel.

When they had finally finished laughing, they checked over the sledge. Remarkably, it was still in one piece.

"I don't believe it," said Liselle. "I was sure it was going to smash into pieces."

"Your brother certainly was good at his carpentry," added Joe.

"Amazing," said Daniel running one of his hands along the polished wood.

"Indeed," said a familiar stern voice from behind them.

Startled, they jumped and turned around to find themselves face to face with the abbot. He had appeared out of nowhere, and there wasn't any sign of footprints. There had always been rumours that the old abbot had the power to translocate, but no one had ever witnessed him doing it. The abbot's Power Bracelet glowed golden red on his left wrist.

"That was incredible," exclaimed Daniel.

"That won't wash with me boy," snapped the old man. "You three are in a lot of trouble. Don't you realise how close the war is getting to us. We can keep you safe in the orphanage, but not out here. If anything were to happen to you, then you would be on your own," said the abbot seriously.

"Now hand it over."

Daniel passed the sledge rope over to the abbot, who fixed him with a level stare.

"I'm not talking about the sledge; but we'll burn it anyway. It will help to keep us all warm during this unusually cold winter."

He turned to Liselle.

"Give me the key," he said.

Liselle opened her mouth as if to argue.

"Don't deny it. I often wondered how your brother managed to leave us so prematurely. It's too much of a coincidence that you were able to get out as well. So you must have a key," he declared confidently. "I'm sure that you don't wish to go through the indignity of being searched now do you?" he added quietly.

Frantically, Liselle fumbled inside her coat and produced the wooden key. Sheepishly, she handed it over to the monk.

"Ah," said the abbot softly, examining the key. "I remember now that your brother was always rather partial to a spot of out of hour's wood working. I think that I shall have to have a quiet word with Brother Bartholomew."

"Six months kitchen duty for you all, I think!" he snapped suddenly.

"Six months!" they exclaimed in unison.

Later, when they had arrived back at the monastery after a long trudge through the thick snow, and without the aid of the sledge, they discussed the morning's events.

"Phew, that was lucky," said Joe.

"I know," said Liselle. "I can't believe he only gave us kitchen duty."

"I felt sure that we would be kicked out," said Daniel.

"We've all got the same punishment, which means that we'll be together still," said Joe.

"Yes that's important. Whatever happens, we should always stay together," said Liselle.

"Why, what do you think is going to happen?" asked Daniel

"Nothing, I just think we need to look out for one another," she replied.

"I agree," said Joe. "Let's make a pact."

Chapter 2
Guardians

The snow had long since melted and spring had revitalised the countryside. Now well into summer, the trees were covered in green leaves and fragrant flowers, and everywhere plants were blooming. In the monastery's kitchen garden, the monks and orphans toiled, tending to the crops they had planted earlier in the year and battling continuously to keep the weeds at bay.

"Remind me again how long we have left doing kitchen duty," said Joe, looking wistfully out through the kitchen window. He glanced down at his hands, which were holding two scrubbing brushes. Most of his blisters had healed over well; the Healing Charm had seen a lot of use over the previous months.

"Two days," answered Liselle, from the sink where she was peeling potatoes.

"Ah yes, I remember now," said Joe grinning.

"I don't know how you could have forgotten. We told you that only an hour ago," complained Daniel, looking up from his position in front of one of the big ovens that he was cleaning. He sat back on his heels to rest.

"And an hour before that too," added Liselle.

"I know, I know, but I just like hearing you say it. It's like music to my ears," said Joe closing his eyes and smiling contentedly as he imagined doing anything but working in the kitchen.

"I'm hungry," said Daniel, interrupting Joe's reverie.

"You're always hungry," stated Joe.

"Well, I'm starving," said Liselle.

"What would you like to eat?" Daniel asked Liselle.

"I'll have an apple please."

"Yes please," added Joe.

"I thought you weren't hungry?" teased Daniel.

"I didn't say any such thing," smiled Joe.

"Go and watch the corridor," ordered Daniel, completely exasperated.

Joe crossed the kitchen and opened the door slightly.

"It's all clear," he whispered loudly back to the other two.

"Why doesn't he announce it to the whole world," whispered Liselle, as Daniel opened the door to the cellars.

Daniel sniggered as he crept silently down the steps that led to the cellar beneath the kitchen.

"Don't forget the loose step," added Liselle quickly, but she was too late. She heard the stone grind as it moved and then a crash, followed by cursing, as Daniel hit the cellar floor. There was a quiet pause followed by the familiar murmur of the Healing Charm and the grinding noise again as Daniel replaced the stone.

Liselle jumped as Joe hissed loudly, "Bart's coming, get him back."

"Daniel, come back, it's Brother Bart," she called down into the cellar.

Joe leapt away from the door as Brother Bartholomew burst through in a rush. The kindly monk was in a terrible state. Sweat poured from his forehead and his face was like thunder. Both Liselle and Joe assumed that they were in serious trouble.

"Quickly, hide," he said to them.

"What, why?" asked Joe in total confusion, looking across at the bewildered Liselle. This was not what they had expected from the monk.

"We're under attack," he answered gravely.

They started to panic; they had always been warned that this day might come but had never really expected it to do happen.

"What should we do?" asked Liselle.

"Quickly now, get in the cellar, you can hide with Daniel."

"How did you know…?" trailed off Joe as the monk ushered them both towards the cellar door, where they met Daniel coming out.

"I heard you say we're under attack. Who from?" he asked.

"The Koronians obviously," snapped Brother Bartholomew, pushing them all through the door.

"Get to the far end. There are some old blankets. Hide under them," he instructed.

"And mind the loose stone," he added, in time for them all to jump over the troublesome step.

Bart closed the door and bolted it shut. They lurched through the darkness, stumbling and falling over objects in their path until they collided with the far wall of the cellar and threw themselves under a heap of musty old blankets.

They could hear noises from the monastery above them, shouting and dull explosions. After a while, the noises stopped, and then they heard the cellar door scrape open noisily. Gruff voices spoke to each other in a harsh tongue that they couldn't understand. One of the voices came closer. They lay completely still, too terrified even to breathe; a heavy man was coming down the steps. There was an inevitable grinding noise as the wobbly step came loose, followed by the usual clatter of a body crashing down the steps. Although the subsequent muttering was in a foreign language, it was not difficult to imagine the sort of words he was uttering. After a short while, they heard him return up the steps and they breathed freely again.

After what seemed like hours, they ventured from under the blankets. All had gone quiet. The cellar door was wide open, letting in enough light to guide them safely across the cellar. Carefully they crept up the steps, and peered cautiously into the kitchen. Clearly, there had been a fight that had involved magic. Most of the furniture in the room had been destroyed and there were black scorch marks everywhere. They could only guess at what kind of deadly magic had caused the damage. Then they saw something that terrified them; on the kitchen floor were the bodies of two of the monks. They knew that the monks were dead; nobody alive would lie in such contorted positions. Moving slowly past the bodies, they listened carefully. They couldn't hear any voices but there was a quiet crackling noise as though a log fire had been lit somewhere in the monastery.

"Look," said Daniel pointing to the top of the doorway that led to the rest of the monastery. Wisps of dark smoke were curling around the top of the doorframe and the crackling sound was getting louder. Venturing a cautious look up the corridor, they could see bright flames licking their way towards them, driving a thick black cloud of smoke along the ceiling.

"They've set fire to the monastery," exclaimed Liselle, unable to believe that anybody was capable of such a wanton act.

"We have to get out," said Joe, "and quickly."

Daniel ran across the kitchen and pulled on the latch of the door that led to the kitchen gardens, the same door that they had crept through early one wintry morning several months ago. Fortunately, the door was unlocked and they tumbled through the doorway, tripping over one another in their haste to escape. Looking back at the door, they could see smoke already coiling around the doorframe, as fresh air rushed through the open door to feed the flames. Great plumes of fire were spouting from the monastery windows and the heat from the fire forced them back away from the burning building.

"I hope there's nobody inside," said Liselle.

"What do we do now?" said Joe helplessly.

"Well, I guess the attackers must have left," said Daniel, "so let's see if anyone else was able to get away."

As they crossed the lawn to the back gate they saw in a corner of the garden the large form of Brother

Bartholomew; he was lying face down in one of the vegetable patch.

"Oh no," moaned Liselle miserably, "not Bart."

They all assumed that the kindly monk was dead like the others in the kitchen, but on hearing them approach, he let out a muffled groan.

"He's alive," said Joe rushing forward and dropping to his knees at the monk's side.

Joining him quickly, Liselle and Daniel helped to roll over the large man, so that he came to rest on his back. His eyes were closed. Liselle gasped and put her hand to her mouth; there was a deep gash across Brother Bartholomew's forehead.

"You saved us Bart," whispered Daniel, leaning forward and wiping away some of soil from the monk's face.

"Joe, try the Healing Charm," suggested Liselle.

"But, I've only ever used it on myself," answered Joe.

"There's nothing to lose," urged Daniel, "he might not survive if we do nothing."

Placing his hands over the injured monk's head, Joe closed his eyes and focused his mind. He muttered the Healing Charm under his breath and continued to concentrate, repeating the charm until the strain became too much.

Joe sat back exhausted. "I've only stopped the bleeding. I think there's far more internal damage," said Joe wiping his brow with the back of his hand.

Bart opened his eyes and looked up at the young healer.

"Thank you Joe, it doesn't hurt as much now. You've helped an old man to die peacefully."

"Brother Bart, tell us what happened please," said Liselle.

"No, leave him to rest," snapped Joe.

"No, no, it's alright Joe. You need to know what happened, so you can help the other children," said Bart softly.

"That's right," said Daniel. "Where are the others? The only bodies that we've seen have been monks."

"I knew that something wasn't right, as soon as I saw him. He was dressed from head to foot in thick leather and furs and his voice had a strange accent," started Bart.

"Who was?" asked Joe gently, as Liselle and Daniel exchanged puzzled looks.

"I listened briefly and then rushed to the hall," continued Bart, as if he hadn't heard. "On the way, I knocked over the Friar. That was when I remembered you three were in the kitchen."

Bart sighed heavily then continued. "They have their own magic, you see. It's fire magic. We didn't stand a chance. We used Repulsion Charms, but their fireballs ricocheted and set the building alight."

Suddenly Liselle put a finger over her lips.

"Hush, I can hear someone coming. Listen," whispered Liselle sharply.

They could hear voices, shouting from round the side of the monastery.

"They must be coming back," said Joe intensely.

"Right then, it's time that we left," said Brother Bartholomew.

"Don't be silly Bart, you're in no condition to move anywhere," said Joe wisely.

"Ah well, maybe not the way you think. Now quickly, hold on tightly," he instructed and reaching for his leg, he clasped his hand around his ankle.

"A Power Bracelet," exclaimed Daniel, noticing for the first time the copper coloured band around the monk's leg.

They all reached forward and put their hands over Brother Bartholomew's hand. The injured monk closed his eyes and began to chant quietly under his breath.

They could hear the crunch of gravel under foot, and then a voice shouted. Suddenly the world blurred and they felt their stomach's lurch violently. In an instant, the monastery and the garden vanished.

Chapter 3
Chance Encounters

"Where are we?" asked Daniel sitting up.

Joe and Liselle had both been sick, and Daniel didn't feel much better. Brother Bartholomew lay unconscious on the ground and looked very pale.

"That's not the best way to travel," moaned Liselle, holding her head in her hands.

"No, but it is probably the quickest," said Joe. His hands were clamped firmly to the sides of his head and he was staring at the ground. "Oh, when will the world stop spinning?" he groaned.

Daniel stood up and looked about him.

"Look there's a farm over there," he said excitedly. "I'll go and get some help. You two wait here and look after Bart."

"Be careful Daniel," warned Joe. "For all we know, we may be in Koronian territory."

"Maybe," replied Daniel dubiously, "although I would have expected to see more mountains or trees. But you're right; I will be careful."

As Daniel set off for the farm, Liselle and Joe lifted their heads up slowly. They could see that Daniel was right. According to their teachers, Koronia was all forest and mountain ranges, yet the country they looked at now was anything but. They were surrounded by low rolling hills, most of which had been turned to farmland. Some fields contained livestock, while others had crops and the remainder lay fallow. The only buildings visible were those of the farm towards which Daniel was heading. They gazed after him as he made his way across the fields and climbed over the stone wall that surrounded the farm. Nervously they watched as Daniel knocked on the door and a figure opened it briefly, before disappearing back inside. Daniel turned and looking back at Liselle and Joe, he gave them a wave. They waved back at him.

"What do you think that means?" asked Joe.

"I think it's a good sign," answered Liselle. "Yes look, there's a man coming out of the farmhouse."

The farmer led Daniel into one of the barns and presently they emerged sitting at the front of a farm cart being pulled by a large horse.

Joe moved closer to Brother Bartholomew. "Bart, can you hear me?" he asked gently.

The monk didn't response, but Joe continued talking. "There's help coming," he said. "Daniel fetched a farmer and he's bringing a cart. We can get you back to the farm and then you can have a good rest."

Daniel and the farmer arrived quickly, and working together, they heaved the monk's large body into the cart. As they returned to the farm, Daniel introduced his friends to the farmer whose name was Col. Discretely, they explained how they had managed to get themselves lost, and were unsure of their exact location. Col didn't say much, but he did tell them where they were.

"We're miles from home," whispered Joe to Liselle.

"What home?" said Liselle quietly.

On their arrival at the farm, they were met by a tall thin kindly looking woman, who greeted them enthusiastically at the front door, and told them her name was Gwen. Immediately, she took charge of the situation and guided the others as they carried Brother Bartholomew into the house, and then, with some difficulty, up the stairs to a small room.

"Now then, everybody out please. I'll see to him," Gwen ordered officiously.

Col left the room immediately, but the others were more reluctant.

Gwen saw their concerned looks, and smiled fondly.

"You needn't look so concerned," she said softly. "He's in good hands now. I won't harm him," she added reassuringly. "You all look like you could do with a rest yourselves, and there's not much more you can do for him." She looked down seriously at the unconscious monk.

Encouraged by Gwen's words and her pleasant demeanour, they left the room and went back downstairs to find Col busy laying out food on the kitchen table. They needed little persuading to join him for supper.

Not long after they had finished eating, Gwen descended the stairs and joined them at the table.

"How is he?" asked Joe seriously. "We thought that he was going to die."

"He might well have done," answered Gwen, "but thanks to you he should make a full recovery. That was a very nasty blow to the head, and he is very lucky to be alive. Was it you that patched up his wound?"

"I just wanted to stop the bleeding," answered Joe.

Gwen nodded in understanding.

"Now don't you go worrying about a thing my dears. He will be quite all right with us. A few weeks of rest are all that he needs now."

They slept soundly that night, whilst the farmer's wife stayed up with Brother Bart, tending to his wounds. They did not wish to impose on the good farmer and his wife so had decided to leave for Southersby the next day.

Gwen allowed them in to Bart's room to say a brief good bye to the man that had saved their lives the day before. The usually cheerful monk was sitting up in bed looking quite despondent, partly due to his injuries, but mostly because of the tragic loss of their friends.

"Goodbye my children. Take care of one another," he said hugging each of them in turn.

Gwen provided them with a pack containing food and water, which they accepted gratefully, and Col gave them directions for Southersby.

"Why are you being so good to Brother Bart?" asked Liselle carefully.

"How could I do anything else? Bartholomew is my little brother," answered Gwen.

"Her little brother!" exclaimed Joe when they were out of earshot of the farmhouse.

"I know, it's not the word that I would have used to describe Brother Bart," giggled Liselle.

"I'm glad I was too surprised to laugh out loud," sniggered Daniel.

"Still, he's a clever bloke that Brother Bart," said Joe admiringly.

Daniel nodded his head vigorously in agreement.

"He managed to translocate all four of us across the country to within a couple of fields of his sister's farm. That takes some doing."

Liselle agreed, and then added, "I wonder why he never mentioned that he had a sister."

Daniel and Joe shrugged their shoulders.

They followed the well-worn and rutted track as it meandered slowly through the rolling hills, passing by farms and through small villages where they were watched suspiciously by the inhabitants. They smiled and waved amiably at the villagers, who let them pass unhindered. As they neared the coastline, the unmistakable salty smell of the sea reached their senses. None of them had ever seen the sea before and the thrill of seeing it for the first time forced them into a run. The track met the coastal road at a junction, exactly as Col had described to them. Large sand dunes hid the sea from view, but they could hear waves crashing onto the beach. Their hearts pounding with excitement, they crossed the coastal road and pulled themselves up the nearest dune using the long grass that grew through the sand. They crested the dune and before them lay a large expanse of beach and beyond that was the clear blue sea.

"It's beautiful," said Liselle, as the cool sea breeze whipped at her hair. The sun reflected off the twinkling water and the rolling waves broke against an outlying reef. Running and falling down the side of the sand dune, they raced to be the first into the water. Joe won easily and stopped just short of the water's edge where he swiftly removed his footwear and waded into the icy water.

"It's freezing," he exclaimed to the others as they removed their own shoes and joined him.

"What do you expect?" asked Liselle. "We've just had winter. The sea needs all summer to warm up properly."

After a short paddle, the cold water forced them to return to the warmth of the sand, where they picked up their shoes and walked bare-footed along the deserted beach. The sand eventually gave way to shingle as the beach narrowed and the sand dunes ended.

"I reckon it's about time we had something to eat," suggested Liselle.

"Good idea," agreed Daniel, looking hungrily at Joe who was carrying the pack.

As they settled down on the beach, they heard a piercing cry, coming from further along the coast.

"What was that?" asked Daniel, coming swiftly to his feet.

"Probably some kind of seabird," answered Joe knowledgably.

"Know a lot about seabirds, do you?" asked Liselle, giving Daniel a sly grin.

Daniel peered into the distance, his hand shielding his eyes from the sun. He could see where the shingle ended and the land rose steeply. Waves crashed against the base of the cliffs.

"Let's take a look," he suggested, putting on his shoes.

"What about lunch?" Joe complained.

Daniel looked down at his friend and smiled.

"Come on," he said. "I think I can see something, and it looks much larger than any seabird that I've read about."

Joe sighed, and put on his own shoes, as did Liselle. They walked quickly towards the cliffs, and soon, they could see more clearly the object that Daniel had spotted.

As they approached, it let out another desperate cry. It was evidently an animal in considerable distress. At the base of the cliffs, they found a large creature trapped under fallen rocks that pinned it in the water. From what they could make out, the being was lizard-like, with long and scaly with a spiny head, four limbs, and a tail equally as long as its body. Each time the waves rolled in, the stricken animal struggled for breath, spluttering as the waters receded.

"We have to help it," said Daniel seriously.

"But what is it?" asked Joe. "It might be dangerous."

"I've heard of these giant lizards, but I thought that they lived in more tropical areas of the world. They can even swim in the sea," said Liselle.

"Maybe it's a dragon," suggested Joe.

"Don't be silly. Dragons don't exist," said Daniel.

"Yes they do," argued Liselle.

"If they did ever exist, then they must have died out a long time ago. I've never met anyone who ever saw a dragon."

"Of course, you've met everybody haven't you?"

"So, are we going to help it or not?" asked Joe, as the lizard let out a pitiful cry. "I don't think it's going to last much longer."

They waded into the knee-deep water, and began pulling away chunks of rock. The giant lizard's eyes watched them with a mixture of fear and hope. Soon, there remained just the one rock, a large flat one that lay across the creature's back. It would take all their strength to move it.

"When the thing's loose, I think we should step back a bit," advised Joe. "I don't like the look of those teeth."

Heaving on the slab of rock, they managed to drag it off the giant lizard's back. The rock crashed into the water, spraying all of them as they jumped back onto the relative safety of the beach.

As soon as the giant lizard was free, it scuttled on all fours out of the sea, and turned to survey its rescuers. As they studied one another, the lizard sat back on its much larger hind legs. It was a lot taller than they were, about the height of a large man. Then from behind its back, the lizard unfurled two large leathery wings and coughed. A small ball of yellow flame flew from its mouth.

"That is definitely not a lizard," said Joe.

The dragon cocked it's head on one side and peered at them.

"He's sort of cute, isn't he," said Liselle.

The boys looked at one another worriedly.

"Er no, not really Liselle," said Joe.

"I think that he must be a baby; look at his little face, he's watching us," said Liselle.

The young dragon turned his head to look at them from a different angle, craning his neck from left to right and peering at them.

"It's probably trying to decide if we're any good to eat," said Daniel.

"Of course," said Liselle suddenly.

Joe took a step back.

"I thought you were joking," he said to Daniel.

"So did I," he replied.

"He's hungry," explained Liselle impatiently. "We'll give him some food."

Joe took another step back, clutching the food bag defensively, and using Liselle as a shield. The dragon stretched its long neck round Liselle and peered hopefully at Joe.

"Not our food," said Joe protectively, moving further around Liselle.

"It can't do any harm to give him a little something," said Daniel.

"Give him a little something? Look at the size of the beast; he'd swallow the whole bagful as soon as look at it," argued Joe.

"Stop being so selfish," said Liselle, quickly snatching the bag away from Joe.

She reached in, pulled out a small pie, and offered it to the dragon on the flat of her hand.

"I was looking forward to that pie," sulked Joe.

The young dragon sniffed hesitantly at Liselle's outstretched palm, then recoiled and looked at them suspiciously.

"Go on," Liselle encouraged the dragon. "Take it, go on, it's nice."

"Take a bite," suggested Daniel.

"Yeah, take a bite of your hand, more likely," grumbled Joe.

Liselle took a small bite of the pie and held it out again.

"You see, it's really good," she said, trying to coax the young dragon to feed.

"Oh great," complained Joe. "Everybody else gets a bite, but not me."

"Shush," hissed Liselle, as the dragon sniffed again at the pie, and then with very gentle lips, it took the pie and swallowed it whole.

"Good boy," said Liselle excitedly, reaching her hand back into the bag.

Joe grabbed the bag back from her. "We have a long way to go. I'm not being selfish; I just want don't wish to starve to death."

"I don't think that you need to worry," said Daniel. "Look, I think he's trying to take off."

The young dragon had turned away from them and stretched out its wings. It was jumping comically from one foot to the other and coughing out fireballs. Eventually, it finished its little dance, and took off, spiralling up into the blue sky.

"We ought to get going. It won't be long until it gets dark, and I for one don't wish to spend the night outside. Not with dragons roaming freely about the place," said Joe, when the dragon had faded into the distance.

"I thought you were hungry," accused Daniel.

"My priorities have been changed for me. Come on," said Joe, running quickly up the beach towards the road.

They had not gone more than half a mile, when above them they heard a terrible screech. Looking up, they saw three large shadows against the sun that looked like giant bats with long tails.

"Too late," said Daniel.

"Uh oh, this doesn't look at all good," added Joe.

Out of the sky swooped three enormous dragons. They landed, surrounding the terrified friends, and towered over them, belching flames of red, gold, and green over their heads. The dragons crouched on huge hind legs, using their great long tails to balance. Their spiny heads twisted and turned as they examined the Daniel, Liselle, and Joe in turn. Long tongues flitted in and out, tasting and smelling the air around them.

The friends cowered before the massive beasts as slowly the dragons encircled them. Then, the red dragon lowered its head alongside Liselle, and snorted. Liselle shook with fear, but the dragon nuzzled her gently, and dropped its shoulder towards her.

"What's he doing?" asked Liselle, her voice quaking as she looked desperately at the boys.

Joe was frozen.

Daniel answered her. "I think he wants you to climb on," he said.

"Daniel, I'm scared," said Liselle, tears welling in her eyes.

"Go on, I think it'll be okay. If they were going to harm us, they'd have done it by now."

"How can you be so sure?" hissed Joe.

"I'm not too sure," answered Daniel calmly. "It's almost as if I can feel their thoughts inside my head. I think they want to thank us for saving the little dragon."

Liselle took a deep breath, and with her heart pounding in her chest, she reached out her arms and took hold. As she tried to pull herself up, the dragon gently placed its clawed foot beneath Liselle and lifted her on. Liselle sat astride the dragon's huge neck, much like sitting on a horse, comfortably seated on his shoulders with her legs hanging down and her hands firmly clasping the spines that ran down the back of its neck. The dragon smelt musky, like very old leather. Liselle felt the dragon's body tense, and then it lurched upwards as its powerful rear legs propelled them into the air. The dragon flapped its great wings, the force of the downdraft knocking Daniel and Joe to the ground, and then the red dragon and Liselle were airborne. They circled low three times around the boys and the other dragons, and with a roar from its throat that nearly shook Liselle from her perch, the red dragon rocketed skywards.

Daniel and Joe pulled themselves to their feet and stared after the rapidly shrinking image of the red dragon. A snort from the green dragon and a playful nudge from the gold dragon in the middle of Joe's back prompted the boys to turn and face their own steeds. The dragons lowered their shoulders, in the same way that the red one had done for Liselle.

"I really don't know about this," said Joe fearfully.

"That's alright," replied Daniel. "You can stay here on your own, and Liselle and I will let you know what it was like later."

Daniel walked towards the head of the green dragon and stroked it down its nose. The dragon closed its eyes contentedly and gave a cat-like purr, which was so loud that it made Daniel's chest vibrate. Daniel smiled at Joe and made his way to the base of the dragon's neck, where he reached up to the spines on its neck, as he had seen Liselle do a few moments earlier.

Daniel looked again at Joe.

"Coming?" he said to his friend, and confidently he pulled himself onto the dragon's back and sat astride the beast's massive shoulders.

"I must be completely mad," muttered Joe, and he took a couple of tentative steps forwards. Before he knew what was happening, the gold dragon had put one toe and claw of its huge foot between Joe's legs and hoisted him effortlessly onto its back, where he sprawled on his front, facing the wrong way.

"Hey, that's not fair," cried Joe, desperately scrambling to face the right way. "If I die, I'm blaming you and Liselle," he yelled at Daniel.

Before Daniel had a chance to reply, the two dragons crouched low, and then lurched into the air almost causing the boys to fall off. The dragons' wings cracked the air, and they too shot upwards.

The green and the gold dragon raced though the sky to catch up the red dragon and Liselle, who were nearly out of sight. Their heads stretched out in front, they strained forwards with every beat of their wings, desperate to join the fleeing dragon and rider. The dragons tucked their legs in neatly along their bodies and their tails trailed behind them.

"Where are we going?" Daniel shouted across to Liselle, when eventually the green and gold dragons came level with the red.

"I don't know," she yelled back, "and I don't care either." She grinned inanely at Daniel.

Daniel looked across at Joe, whose face was stretched into a mad grin. The dragons flew three abreast, heading north towards the mountains through the warm summer's evening.

Suddenly, they dropped like stones from their great height, and the ground appeared to race up to meet them. The dragons started to play. In mock battle, they lunged at one another, pulling away at the last second steering clear of any collision. Circling around behind, they veered sharply attempting to outwit each other. At times, they dived towards the ground, pulling up at the last instant.

Flying incredibly low and at such speed, often it seemed as though they would crash into a cliff or large tree, but all the while, the deft skill of the ancient dragons avoided all obstacles. Sometimes they surged ahead under a ponderous steady wing beat and sometimes they glided effortlessly. Their wingtips brushed the surface of lakes and casually they trailed their feet, knocking snow from the treetops.

Evening turned quickly into night. They climbed up through the clouds and saw a night sky filled with stars. As the moon rose, it shone brightly and they glided silently above the clouds. Their dark shadows weaved up and down over the moon bright clouds below them, and through gaps in the clouds, they could see the dark land.

Through the night they flew, crossing unknown lands below them, until suddenly it seemed that all too soon it was over. Together the three dragons alighted gently and dropped their shoulders. Daniel, Joe, and Liselle slid from the backs of the giant beasts, and stood facing them sadly, but filled with wonder.

They noticed that all three dragons were wearing single bright bracelets on their smallest toes, which they each let slip to the ground. They were decorated with scales that shimmered and moved as if alive.

"Are they for us?" asked Liselle, picking up the red bracelet dropped by the red dragon.

Daniel and Joe followed suit, respectively collecting the green and gold bracelets.

"They'll never stay on, they're far too loose," complained Joe as they slid them over their wrists.

The bracelets shrunk instantly with a snap and fitted their wrists perfectly.

"Nobody will ever be able to steal this now," said Daniel, tugging at his bright green bracelet. There was no way that it was going to come off.

"Not without chopping off your arms," said Liselle.

Joe and Daniel laughed, and then saw that Liselle was looking serious. Their faces paled, as they understood the implications of their newly acquired treasures. However, as fast as the colour had drained from them, the same happened to the bracelets until they were left wearing dull ordinary looking cheap jewellery. A scaly motif was subtly visible, but it could just as easily have been poor polishing.

"Oh well, I knew it was too good to last," said Joe.

"I'm relieved," said Liselle. "I wouldn't want anyone trying to remove it."

"I guess it was simply an illusion. I have heard that dragons are capable of great magic," said Daniel. He looked up at the green dragon, whose bright emerald green eyes sparkled as it looked at him in a way that suggested as though the dragon could understand his every word. "Thank you," said Daniel gratefully.

Gently the dragons nuzzled the three friends and allowed them to stroke their heads. Then, sadly, they pushed the three friends away with their noses, and one by one, the great beasts took off. The last to leave was the gold dragon, which kept looking back forlornly at Joe until they disappeared over the hills.

"We can never tell anyone about this," said Daniel.

"The most amazing thing to ever happen to us and you want me to keep quiet. No way!" spluttered Joe.

"I didn't think the ride was very comfortable," said Liselle.

"All you ever do is moan," teased Joe.

"It beats translocation any day," said Daniel.

"I'm hungry," complained Liselle.

"You're always hungry," responded Joe.

"Well aren't you hungry?"

"No I'm not as it happens. Actually I'm starving."

"Well, where are we anyway?"

"I think that we're about eight miles west of Southersby," said Liselle looking around them.

"No way," exclaimed Joe. "How do you know that?"

"I'm just clever, that's all," she said knowingly and set off along the road.

They hadn't gone more than five steps when Daniel said, "Hey look there's a signpost. It says, 'Southersby, 8 miles.'"

The boys looked at each other, and then at Liselle who was slowly disappearing around the next corner.

"Hey Liselle, who says you're clever?" called out Daniel.

"I do," she yelled back, laughing.

"Quickly, after her! That girl needs to be taught a lesson," said Joe, but Liselle was already running.

Chapter 4
Different Ways

They entered the town of Southersby through the west gate. Although not particularly large, Southersby was a garrison town and as such, it had a permanent military presence. The town was fortified heavily with a high stone wall surrounding most of the buildings and a small barracks at the east gate housed the troops.

On entering the town, they were stopped as they passed under the archway. A self-important looking soldier barred their way, drawing his short sword.

"Where are you from?" snapped the soldier.

They told him of the attack on the monastery and of how they evaded capture by hiding in the cellar.

"But I know that no-one escaped. I headed up the patrol that was sent to investigate yesterday. We found nothing but dead monks and all the orphans kidnapped," said the soldier savagely. "We scoured the countryside for survivors and found no-one. Anyway, how come you have arrived by the west gate? The road from Crickle should bring you to the east gate."

They were unwilling to tell the soldier about how Brother Bartholomew had translocated all of them to safety and their subsequent flight across the country by dragon, so they shrugged their shoulders.

"I guess we must have got lost," suggested Daniel cheekily.

Liselle sniggered, and the officious soldier turned to face her directly. "What's wrong with you?" he asked pointing at her with his sword.

"Sorry, just a touch of hay fever," she answered, covering her smirk with her hand.

Daniel and Joe also covered their mouths to hide their smiles; the guard eyed them suspiciously.

"Well, whatever it is, it better not be catching," he warned them, taking a step away from them.

"Wait here," he said and entered the guardroom, leaving the friends sniggering.

"What if they send us away?" said Joe worriedly.

They looked nervously at one another, concerned that their cheek was not going to help them. The soldier returned with another in tow, whom he instructed to stand guard at the gate.

"It's an unlikely story, but one that you can repeat to the Captain of the Guard," said the bossy soldier. "Now, come with me."

He turned about and marched away quickly. They fell into line behind him. Swinging their arms in childish imitation, they followed the guard across the town to the barracks by the east gate. The townsfolk took plenty of amusement at the expense of the arrogant soldier, with his young mocking followers, who often had to skip or run to keep up with his brisk pace. However, it did not take them very long to reach the other side of the small town. They entered the barracks, where the soldier led them down clean white corridors until they arrived at an open door. He halted abruptly and saluted smartly to the room's occupant.

"Wait here," he instructed them and entered the room.

They listened to the soldier making his report, but were unable to hear the other person, who they assumed to be the Captain of the Guard. Daniel peered round the door in an attempt to get a better look, but all he could see was the soldier's straight back.

"Yes sir, at once," said the soldier. Then he saluted again and turned towards the door as Daniel quickly pulled back his head and leaned against the wall of the corridor.

"Right you three, inside, quick march," ordered the soldier.

They filed past him into the small office and lined up in front of the desk.

"Halt," cried the soldier, following them back in.

"Thank you Corporal, it's quite alright; they're not soldiers remember, and nor are they prisoners, are they?" said the man behind the desk.

"No sir, of course they're not," he replied tentatively, "I just thought that given the situation, you know."

"Okay, thank you Corporal," said the officer, dismissing the soldier, who after hesitating slightly, turned about and marched noisily from the building. Clearly, he had expected to stay and watch them being interrogated.

"Don't worry about him," said the captain turning back to them, and smiling kindly. "He's up for promotion, and wants to appear thorough. He's a good man, if a little pompous, so I think he'll get his promotion soon enough." He studied them briefly then added softly, "Now, more importantly, what brings you to our little town?"

They told him who they were and then, between the three of them, they repeated their story to the captain, and all the while, the captain nodded encouragingly. When they had finished their tale, they fell silent, awaiting their fate.

"Well, all I can say is that the corporal did the right thing by bringing you to me with your story," he said seriously. "I think that you are very lucky to have escaped. Now I won't pretend to believe all that you have told me; there are definitely a few gaps.

"I'm very sorry to hear about your friends and your tutors. We never expected an attack of this sort. We can only assume the Koronians came through the mountains; it is most unusual.

"There is one problem however that you may be able to help me to solve. Our young corporal, who you have recently had the pleasure of meeting," he said light-heartedly to the smiling friends, "headed up the patrol that checked out the monastery yesterday. I think that you may know that already, yes?"

They nodded their agreement, eager to appear helpful.

"He really is very thorough, is our corporal, and he managed to account for every monk except one. He did however find evidence of somebody who had been badly injured, but has since vanished.

"He thinks that Brother Bartholomew may have helped the attackers, and they took him with them when they left, and that you three know this and are trying to protect him by not providing us with a complete picture," he said quietly.

"He would never have done so, that's a lie," defended Joe, "if it hadn't been for Bart, we'd have been captured. He was the one that saved us."

Daniel and Liselle sighed.

"Thank you Joe," said the Captain kindly. "Perhaps you would be good enough to continue."

Joe stuttered and looked apologetically at his friends, who shrugged their shoulders. It was too late to come up with a new story.

"Please Joe, do go on," urged the officer, smiling encouragingly. "I believe you were about to tell me how Brother Bartholomew translocated each of you in turn to somewhere safe. Is my assumption correct Joe?"

"Not quite, he didn't translocate us in turn; we all went together," said Joe admiringly.

"But surely that's not possible, is it?"

The officer looked to Daniel and Liselle for some support to his question, but they shook their heads, smiling as they did. They liked the idea that Bart had defeated the impossible.

Joe explained how they had found the injured monk, through to their arrival at the farm of Brother Bartholomew's sister.

"And how far away is this farmhouse?"

"Oh, not too far from the sea," answered Joe.

Daniel and Liselle stiffened as they could see what was coming. Joe, still wrapped up in his admiration for Brother Bartholomew's Charms skills, ploughed on blindly with their story.

"That's an incredibly long way to translocate," said the Captain. "However did you get back so quickly?"

Joe was about to answer, than faltered, finally hit by the realisation of what he was about to reveal. They all looked at each other hesitantly.

"All right, don't tell me if you don't wish to. You're safe, that's what's important. More charms I guess," he smiled at them.

"Something like that," said Liselle quickly.

"Why are you all wearing the same bracelet?" he asked suddenly.

"They were given to us at the monastery; we all wear them," answered Daniel.

The captain looked doubtfully at each of them in turn, and then smiled broadly.

"If you say so," he said.

Much to their surprise, the Captain then showed them to the mess hall. It was a narrow room with long tables and benches, not unlike the dining room at the monastery. Dinner was nearly over and the only occupants were some late stragglers, who were dotted around the room. They collected their meals from a service hatch, through which they could see the kitchen. A skinny man wearing white clothes and a tall white hat served them and encouraged them to come back if they wanted any more when they had finished.

"Do you think he eats any of his own food; he's so thin?" whispered Liselle as they shuffled onto the end of a table.

"He doesn't offer much confidence in the quality of his own food," agreed Joe.

"It tastes alright though," mumbled Daniel through a full mouthful.

Despite their initial reservations, they all ate quickly and returned to the hatch for more, where the thin cook was all too eager to refill their empty plates.

"So what do we do now?" asked Joe as he finished, sitting back contentedly from the table and resting his back on the wall behind him.

Daniel, who was sitting opposite, leaned forward with his chin on his hands.

"Well, we can't stay here, that's obvious. I would like to go back to the monastery," he said.

"Why bother, it sounds like there's nothing left there," said Joe.

"I'd like to find my brother," said Liselle sadly. "I haven't heard from him for a little while and he may have heard about what has happened to the monastery. I ought to let him know that I'm alright."

"You should ask the Captain. If you tell him your brother's unit, he might have a list or something that will say where he is," suggested Daniel.

Liselle brightened up considerably.

"Thanks Daniel, that's a really good idea," she said gratefully.

"And I want to let my mother know that I'm alright, then see if my father is still alive somewhere," said Joe.

"What about you Daniel?" asked Liselle. "Why do you want to return to the monastery? It's like Joe said, there's nothing left."

"I've already lost both my parents to this war and now I've lost the only place that I could ever really call home. You two and Bart are all that I have left, but I would like to know what happened to the others from the monastery."

Liselle and Joe looked embarrassed. They had forgotten about their friends who had been captured.

"So much has happened," Joe started to say.

"There's no excuse really," said Liselle. "I can't believe that we've been so selfish. We were very lucky."

"Luck had nothing to do with our escape. It was Brother Bart. He saved our lives," said Joe.

"Maybe we should go with you?" offered Liselle.

"That's alright Liselle. You and Joe both have family who you need to find. If I was in the same situation as you, I would want to find my brother," he said looking at Liselle. "Or my missing father," he added turning to Joe.

"Still, you shouldn't go on alone really. There could be more Koronians about," argued Liselle.

"I'll start by going back to the monastery and I'll talk to the villagers at Crickle. I'm not going to just march straight East until I find them. I'm not that stupid," said Daniel bluntly.

"But that silly Corporal will have already checked all that," said Joe. "Why don't you come with me to find my parents, or at least go with Liselle? You know she'll be lost without us."

"I'm sure I'll manage perfectly fine by myself," retorted Liselle indignantly. "Although I would be happy to have you along Daniel," she added quickly.

They all fell quiet again, each wrapped up in their own thoughts. Daniel was the first to notice the feint smiles appearing on the faces of Liselle and Joe; clearly, they were imagining the same thing as he was.

"I can't stop thinking about the dragons," he whispered.

"Oh I know," said Liselle softly, seemingly desperate to share her thoughts. "I would love to fly again; just one more time."

"I know what you mean," agreed Joe wistfully. "Every thought I have is filled with dragons."

Their conversation was interrupted by the Captain of the Guard, who had returned to the mess hall. They explained their decisions to the Captain and he nodded approvingly although he showed some concern over Daniel's decision to return to the monastery.

"I'm afraid that your friends will be well on their way to the Koronian city of Thraldom, there to be used as slave labour in the kitchens," he said sadly.

"I understand that, but I want to check for myself. It may be that some of the younger ones managed to find somewhere to hide, but were too scared to come out when they saw your men," said Daniel.

The Captain relented, and then showed them to a small building that was empty except for a few bunk beds, where they were to sleep. They all slept soundly that night, their dreams filled with images of gold, red, and green fire and the thrill of the wind in their faces as they flew low over mountains and streams.

All too soon, morning arrived, interrupting their dragon filled dreams. After a hearty breakfast, complete with several return trips to the serving counter and the happy cook, the Captain of the Guard took them to the barracks food store and kitted them out with a week's worth of provisions. He also supplied each of them with an army backpack and a blanket for the nights. He had checked his personnel details and provided them with some information on the location of Liselle's brother and Joe's mother. His records were not very up to date, but he was quite sure that Liselle would find Charlie in Calistan, the country's capital city. He confirmed that Joe's mother was working as a nurse at one of the hospital towns and showed him where on a map. They thanked him graciously; he had already done so much for them. When they were ready to leave, he accompanied them as far as the east gate, where a small cavalry detachment was preparing to leave.

"Take care all of you, and stick to the roads," he advised them. "After the attack on the orphanage I don't need to tell you all to be very careful out there. I'm taking a big risk in letting you go on alone, but I can see that you're all sensible enough not to do anything silly."

They all said their goodbyes and then as they passed under the stone archway of the east gate, the Captain called out to them, "One last thing before you leave us; we've been hearing some very strange rumours concerning sightings of dragons'. I don't suppose you saw anything strange yesterday before you came into town, did you?"

They all shook their heads, and then they set off quickly along the dusty road leaving the town of Southersby behind them. They walked in silence for most of the morning until they reached the crossroads where they were to part ways. They had passed a couple of empty villages and had seen very few travellers on the road. The mounted soldiers they had seen getting ready to leave Southersby had overtaken them not long after their own departure.

"I quite liked that Captain," said Liselle, when they arrived at the crossroads.

Joe and Daniel agreed. "Do you think he suspected something?" asked Joe. "Like his question about the dragons just as we were leaving."

Liselle and Daniel nodded together. "I think he was very suspicious," answered Daniel, "but you're right, I liked him all the same."

They fell silent again for a while, looking about them at the four roads that met at the crossroads. The road to Southersby lay to the west and the road that would take Daniel back to Crickle and the burnt out monastery led northwest. To the northeast was a rough track that wound away through the low hills to the castles and watchtowers on the border. Directly south was the route that Liselle and Joe were to follow in the search for their families.

"I guess this is it then; now we go our separate ways," said Liselle, eventually breaking the awkward silence.

"So much for our pact about not splitting up. I thought we agreed that we would never become separated," said Joe sadly.

"I know, but the war has changed all of that," explained Daniel as a lump started to swell in his throat.

"Do you think we'll ever see each other again?" asked Liselle quietly.

"Definitely," replied Daniel, coughing to clear his throat. "It may not be for some time to come, but one day this stupid war will end. Then nothing will be able to stop us from getting back together.

"Of course, Joe will probably have a wife and three children by then," he added laughing. "Look, I'm sure that it won't be for long. As soon as I've had a good look for the others, I'll come looking for you two again. It'll be a week at most, I'm certain of it," said Daniel positively.

"I suppose so," said Liselle dubiously.

"Well, what's the worst that can happen?" asked Joe cheerfully.

"I don't think we want to answer that one," replied Liselle solemnly.

They said their goodbyes as happily as they could, each of them masking a feeling of foreboding that they could feel in their stomachs. They had all been together for so long that the thought of being apart made them nervous. With a final farewell, Joe and Liselle turned towards the south and set off along the road that they hoped would take them closer to their families.

Daniel waited until they were out of sight, then crossed the road and marched due East towards the border.

Chapter 5
Joe and Liselle

"You don't think he'll do anything foolish do you?" Liselle asked Joe after they had walked a short distance.

"No of course not, he's the sensible one remember?" replied Joe.

"Since when? As I recall, he was the one that insisted we should try out the sledge when it snowed," argued Liselle.

"That's true," agreed Joe. "Don't worry though; I'm sure that he'll be fine."

"Why don't I feel very reassured?" muttered Liselle.

They walked on in silence, each lost in their own thoughts. It had always been the three of them, and now without Daniel they experienced a new sense of loss.

The road they followed meandered through the rolling countryside, mostly following the valley bottoms. The border was only a few miles to the east and most of the villages through which they passed were empty. Some of them showed evidence of fighting and often there was nothing left but the burnt out remnants of the villagers' homes. Occasionally they encountered soldiers or cavalry, many of which overtook them as they were also heading southwards. As dusk approached, they arrived at a deserted village. Finding a door unlocked, they let themselves into a house that appeared to be in reasonable condition.

"There's not much point sleeping outside when we can have a perfectly good roof over our heads," said Liselle, justifying their intrusion on the premises.

"I know," agreed Joe, following Liselle into the little cottage, "but it really doesn't feel right. After all, this is still someone's home. Just because they're not here doesn't make me feel any better about breaking in."

They sat at the wooden table in the kitchen, where they ate a meagre meal, neither of them feeling particularly hungry despite their long walk. When they had finished eating, they sat in silence watching through the window as the sun sank behind the hills to the west.

As darkness engulfed the quiet little village, Joe spoke.

"I wonder where all the troops we saw today were going," he mused aloud.

"I was thinking about that earlier," replied Liselle. "They were all heading in the same direction; going the same way as us."

"Should that worry us or make us feel safe?" asked Joe chuckling.

"Good question," laughed Liselle. "Of course we may find out tomorrow. And speaking of which, I think I'm ready for bed."

Joe was quite happy to let Liselle sleep in the only bed, contented enough to sleep on the wooden floor with only a couple of blankets.

"Using someone else's house is one thing, but I'm not about to start sleeping in their beds as well," he explained to Liselle.

They lay awake for a short while, both thinking the same, hoping that Daniel was safe and worrying a little about the following day when they too would part company. They fell asleep soon enough and slept soundly, their dreams once again full of exhilarating rides on fire-breathing dragons.

It was evident the following morning that it had rained heavily during the night. Joe and Liselle woke early, washed, and ate breakfast. On seeing the wet ground outside, Joe admitted that Liselle had been right to suggest they find a decent place for the night.

"How was the floor?" asked Liselle, mockingly.

"The floor was just fine thank you very much," answered Joe flatly. "Don't push your luck."

Liselle grinned at him and tidied up the kitchen, as Joe checked their packs. Whilst Liselle was in the bedroom making up the bed, Joe removed some of the cured meat from his pack and slipped it into Liselle's. He hoisted his backpack onto his back and went outside to wait. He didn't have to wait long and Liselle appeared at his side with her pack slung loosely over one shoulder. Joe eased the slack strap over her shoulder.

"It was fine where it was," complained Liselle.

"It was fine where it was if you want to develop a hump on your back and spend the rest of your life walking around hunched over like a deformed animal," answered

Joe, bending forewords and swinging his arms ape-like as he walked away.

"All right, fair enough," cried Liselle laughing at Joe's absurd impression.

She closed the door of the little cottage, which had been their home for the night and ran to catch up with Joe, who was walking up the muddy road.

They walked on in silence for most of the morning, following the winding road, pushing ever southward towards the junction where they would separate and pursue their own routes. Like the day before, they passed deserted villages and occasionally saw troops, most of whom overtook them on horseback.

"Do you think Daniel managed to find shelter last night?" Joe eventually asked Liselle.

"He should have reached Crickle before nightfall, and I'm sure somebody there would have put him up for the night. At the very least, he would have been able to sleep in a barn or a shed," she replied reassuringly.

"That's true," said Joe, brightening up a little. "I was thinking about him last night when it was raining, and was worried that he might have been caught out in the open."

"You worry too much," criticised Liselle. "Why did you wake up last night, didn't you sleep very well?"

"I slept soundly enough. I think I woke up momentarily when the rain started," answered Joe. "Normally I sleep really well; at least I have done for the past couple of nights," he said smiling at Liselle.

"Do you dream much?" she asked, inquiringly.

"Oh yes, plenty," said Joe laughing, "and I think you do as well. In fact, I haven't been able to think about much else, and all that I dream about is one day flying again. Do you think it might ever happen?"

Liselle nodded her head vigorously," I'll go mad if we don't. For some reason I just know that one day we'll see dragons again."

"I understand exactly what you're saying; I can feel it in my bones, almost as if they are a part of me."

"Some people say that dragons can do magic; maybe we've been affected by it?"

Their joyful conversation was brought to an abrupt halt; they had arrived at a junction in the road.

"I turn right here," said Liselle looking westwards.

"And I go left," added Joe, looking at the east road.

They delayed their departures by sharing a last meal together. Liselle soon found the extra food that Joe had put in her pack, and looked at him questioningly.

"You've got further to go," he explained.

"Not that much further," argued Liselle, "and besides which, we both have more than enough to get us to our destinations."

Liselle split the cured meat in two and handed half to Joe, who took it reluctantly.

"True, but anything could happen. It's better to be safe than sorry," he said.

"My mother used to say that," said Liselle smiling fondly.

"Sorry," said Joe, "I didn't mean to remind you of anything sad."

"It's alright, you didn't. I enjoy thinking about my parents. I never want to forget them, so memories like this are a good thing."

"And you'll be seeing your brother in a day or two," said Joe, trying to lift the mood.

"And you may see your mother again later today."

"I know," said Joe, grinning. "I'm really excited."

They finished their meal and said goodbye as cheerfully as they could, both of them boosted by the food and optimistic conversation. Despite parting from one another and from Daniel, they both had something to look forward to. Joe promised to follow on after Liselle as soon as he could, doubting that he would be allowed to stay in a town so close to the border for very long, and it was unlikely that there would be any news about his father's whereabouts.

With a final wave, they turned their backs on one another and set off in opposite directions. Liselle headed westwards towards Calistan, and Joe went east in the direction of the border.

Chapter 6
Calistan

The road to Calistan was well maintained and especially straight. Liselle made good time and entered the city through the North Gate on the evening of the second day of her separation from Joe. Her trip had been uneventful. There were many more travellers on this road, all of them moving away from the border, and Liselle had joined a small group of refugees who were fleeing from the fighting. The group had consisted of two families with horse drawn carts and Liselle gratefully accepted a place in one of the carts.

A recent attack by a Koronian raiding party had displaced the families. The marauders had surprised them late at night and set fire to all of the buildings in the village. Fortunately, there were few casualties. The Koronians had allowed the terrified villagers to flee into the surrounding hills. Nervously, the villagers had returned the next day to salvage what little of their possessions remained and then dispersed in search of friends and relatives that might have room for them.

In turn, Liselle told them of the attack on the monastery. The refugees were horrified at Liselle's description of the brutal attack on the monks. None of them could understand why the Koronians would attack peace-loving monks or why they took the orphans captive.

"What I don't understand is how they managed to get past our watchtowers on the border," said one of the refugees.

"Or how they could have returned East with a load of children in tow," added another.

All of them agreed that the war had taken a nasty turn for the worse. Perhaps now would be the time for a major offensive. Surely, their own superior soldiers with their cavalry and armour would defeat the Koronians easily. Liselle wondered how simple villagers could know so much about winning wars and quietly she thought that if the war could been won so easily, then it would all have been over a very long time ago. She decided to keep her thoughts on the subject to herself, doubting that the villages would receive her ideas very well.

The weather at least had improved considerably, and the roads had dried out. By the time that they reached Calistan, all trace of the previous rainwater had evaporated or drained away.

Calistan was huge, much larger than Liselle had expected. Somewhat daunted by all the streets and the large crowds, she gladly went with one of the families to a church used as temporary accommodation for those displaced by the war. The following morning she took leave of her companions to search for the army barracks, where she hoped to find her brother.

The city dwellers were grim faced, not at all like country people. Liselle gave them the benefit of the doubt, since they were all obviously worried about the war. Small groups huddled together on street corners, complaining about the state of the country and spreading terrible rumours about the Koronians. Liselle had to hide her smile when she heard one party discussing the latest tall story about how the Koronians had used dragons to attack a monastery in the north.

Eventually, after many wrong turns, some down rather nasty looking alleyways, and getting directions from reluctant passers by, she arrived at the barracks. There was a very long queue outside the personnel office. She waited all day before the clerk was able to see her, as one by one the people in front of her asked after their own husbands, brothers, or sons. Fortunately, the clerk did know where Liselle could find Charlie, but unhappily, he was not in Calistan. His unit had been posted a few days earlier to a border town to the south east of the city.

Dejectedly, Liselle left the barracks only to find that it was already dark outside. She started to worry; the city streets had little lighting and Liselle did not particularly wish to attempt returning to the church in the dark. She thought about Daniel and Joe and hoped that they were having more luck with their own quests.

Luckily, for Liselle, a passing soldier had seen her concerned face, and on inquiring if she was lost, escorted her to another converted place for refugees. Rather than a church, this refugee centre was a very large and near derelict old mansion. Liselle found a quiet corner, well away from a particularly noisy family, and after a quick meal, she lay down to sleep. Lying on her back, she looked at the stars through the holes in the roof and was glad that the night was clear; she did not fancy sleeping in a puddle of water.

Waking early the following morning, Liselle slipped silently out of the refuge. She made better progress across the near empty city and made fewer mistakes than the day before. Merchants, who had set up their stalls early, seemed happier in the early morning and obligingly gave her directions.

By mid morning, Liselle had arrived at a large gate in the southeast wall of Calistan. The gate was closed, and she had to explain to the sentry where she was going. He accepted her story and allowed her to pass through a small door to the side of the main gate. Clearly, he did not suspect Liselle of being a spy and so was content enough to let her go. The sentry explained how restrictions on travel were being tightened, but was unable to give Liselle the reason why.

Back on the road once more, Liselle was getting used to her own company, and although she thought often of Daniel and Joe, she felt more confident about travelling by herself. Disappointed though she was about not finding her brother in Calistan, she at least knew that she had received positive information about his current location, and would see Charlie very soon.

By late afternoon, Liselle arrived at a typically abandoned village, where she managed to find a small croft that had not been burned down. After a cold meal from her backpack, she went to bed and slept soundly, dreaming her usual wonderful dreams.

The following morning, after she had eaten, Liselle cleaned up, removing any trace of her presence from the little home, and set off along the dusty road. She had not gone far when she was overtaken by a lone horseman in uniform. The soldier looked down at Liselle as he passed and she smiled up at him.

"Where are you going?" enquired the rider, slowing his horse, which tossed its head at the inconvenience.

Cautiously, Liselle explained that she was on her way to see her brother. The man had a kind face, but Liselle was still wary. Careful not to give her brother's name, she described him instead, telling the soldier how her brother was also in the army.

"I think that I know him," said the rider smiling. "You're talking about our Charlie aren't you? He's a corporal in the same unit as me, and I'm heading that way now."

Liselle finally returned his smile, relieved that the man appeared to be genuinely friendly.

"I'll give you a lift if you like," he said, offering his hand.

As he leaned towards Liselle, the horse shifted its weight, preventing Liselle from grasping the soldier's hand, and almost throwing its rider in the process. The soldier righted himself and apologised to Liselle.

"I'm afraid that he's rather a temperamental beast," he explained, "but he's really quite nice when you get to know him."

Liselle took a hesitant step forward, and the horse made as if to bite her; she jumped back quickly.

"Maybe it would be better if I walked the rest of the way. But thank you for your offer," she said.

"Oh no, we'll not be beaten that easily, and certainly not by some silly horse," said the soldier, jumping down from his very smug looking horse.

He walked alongside Liselle for a short way. Eventually, he whispered in Liselle's ear, and she nodded in understanding.

The soldier stopped walking and said, "Well it was nice to have met you."

"Yes, goodbye," replied Liselle, continuing along the road away from the horse and his rider.

The soldier remounted and pushed into a slow trot. Passing very close to Liselle, the horse whinnied and tossed his head arrogantly. No sooner had he done so, then Liselle reached out her arm again, and swiftly the soldier scooped her up and sat her lightly behind him. The horse whinnied indignantly in protest, but did not buck, all too aware that he had been outsmarted.

"Of course, he'll sulk for the rest of the journey," said the soldier laughing, and Liselle smiled contentedly. It would not be long now before she would see her brother again.

They chatted amiably and the time passed rapidly as they covered mile after mile along the well-worn route. They stopped briefly for lunch, before remounting, which the horse consented too, with only a small toss of his mane, and by nightfall, they had arrived at the border town. After a cursory glance from the guard at the gate, they were admitted to the town. Liselle's companion thanked the guard cheerfully, and was rewarded with a small grunt.

"You'll find that gates are often guarded by the most miserable types," he whispered to Liselle as they rode past the guard, who threw Liselle a rather dirty look as she sniggered.

"I need to report in," he explained, "but I'll drop you off at a place where you can stay for the night. Then tomorrow, I'll take you to the barracks, they'll be sure to know where you can find Charlie."

A short way into the deserted town, they stopped at an inn, the only place still occupied, as everyone else had fled to Calistan or beyond. Leaving the horse tied outside, they entered the bar, which was crowded with noisy soldiers who were trying to forget for one evening that they were at war. Liselle was introduced to a large burly woman behind the bar, who rushed round to greet her warmly. The soldier explained Liselle's reason for her journey and subsequent presence in the war-torn town.

"Don't you worry about a thing my love," said the barwoman tenderly, wrapping one great arm around Liselle's shoulders, and squeezing her tightly. "We'll look after you tonight, and tomorrow we'll find your Charlie. We all know Charlie; he was in here only yesterday, so he won't be far away."

Liselle was relieved to hear it, and all of a sudden, she felt very tired, as the weight of worry eased from her shoulders. The soldier saw Liselle's yawn and said that it was time for him to go. Liselle thanked him profusely, and added that she would be very glad to see him again in the morning as he had suggested. As he bade them goodnight and left the inn, Liselle realised that, throughout the entire day, she had not once asked the soldier for his name. Feeling decidedly guilty, she promised herself that she would ask him first thing in the morning, after she had apologised for not having done so already.

The barwoman explained to Liselle that she was in fact the innkeeper, ever since the loss of her husband during a particularly brutal assault by the Koronians two years ago. She had run the place by herself, with only a skeleton crew of staff to assist in the kitchen and the stable. Liselle was shown to a small table in a corner close to the bar, where gratefully she accepted a seat from a young soldier who was on his way out. She looked around nervously at the rest of the men in the room, some of whom were looking her way and laughing. The barwoman reached over the bar and placed a mug on the table in front of Liselle. She took a large gulp, which caused her to cough, and the drink made her throat burn, but it also made her feel more relaxed.

Liselle quickly learnt the kindly barwoman's name, as there were constant cries such as, "Maud, more beer over here please," or "Another bottle this way Maud, if you would be so kind."

Despite their polite speech, Liselle thought that the soldiers in the bar were perhaps not as sincere as they appeared. After all, thought Liselle, there was nothing to stop them from walking up to the bar to order their drinks; they didn't have to yell across the room.

Meanwhile, Maud had disappeared into the kitchen behind the bar, but returned promptly with a plate of food for Liselle.

"I'm afraid I don't have any money," explained Liselle, looking up at Maud apologetically.

"Oh don't be so silly, my dear. I wouldn't take it even if you did," said Maud, embracing Liselle once more with one of her powerful arms. "It's a pleasure having you here.

We haven't seen anybody as young as you for a long time," she added sadly.

Maud left Liselle to her meal, returning to her bar work and the ceaseless orders from the soldiers. Liselle wondered if she might be able to work in the inn, so that she could be close to Charlie. In addition, it would be a way for her to repay the kindness shown to her by Maud. Liselle decided that she would sleep on the idea then enquire in the morning.

Once Liselle had finished her meal and the rest of her drink, which had left her feeling extremely sleepy, Maud showed her to a small but neat room above the bar. Liselle could hear raucous laughter emanating from the room below.

"I'm afraid it's not much," explained Maud, conscious of the boisterous revellers, "but all of the other rooms are already taken by soldiers looking for a night away from the barracks."

"Please don't apologise, I'm really very grateful," said Liselle. "And don't worry about the noise; I'll be asleep in no time at all."

"All right then my dear. Well good night and sleep well," said Maud and quietly she pulled the door closed.

True to her word, Liselle fell asleep as soon as she lay down her head; she had not even bothered to undress.

Liselle dreamt happily about flying over a heavy sea on the back of a red dragon, which swooped and dived with the waves. Alongside her, were the green and gold dragons, with Daniel and Joe astride their great backs, waving and cheering gleefully.

Suddenly she was aware of strong arms, shaking her roughly. As she slowly awoke, she could still hear the crackling of the dragon's flames from her dream.

"Come on Liselle, wake up," said a woman's voice. "Oh, I knew I shouldn't have given you that drink."

Liselle sat up in confusion, unable to recall where she was or whose voice was talking. Opening her eyes drowsily, she finally recognised Maud, who immediately pulled Liselle from her bed. Liselle abruptly became wide-awake; something clearly was very wrong. She could hear voices in the corridor outside her room, and strange large shadows rushed past her open door.

"What is it? What's the matter?" she asked.

"The building is on fire," explained Maud, rushing towards the door, and dragging Liselle with her.

"Oh, not again," cried Liselle.

Liselle realised that the sound of the flames that she thought were part of her dream were, in fact, very real. The far end of the corridor was already ablaze, but Liselle did not have time to look as Maud pulled her down the stairs and safely through the bar and out onto the street. They were the last occupants to escape from the building. Liselle stood and watched, hypnotised by the flames that were gradually engulfing the inn. This was the second time in as many weeks that she had been in a blazing building, and it was the second time that she had had a narrow escape.

Suddenly, she was broken from her trance-like state by shouts coming from the stables. A soldier was leading two horses from the burning building. Passing them to another bystander, he plunged back into the stables, closely followed this time by two more soldiers. They had not been in long when the stable doorway gave way and crashed to the floor where it continued to burn unabated.

Convinced that the brave men would now perish inside the blazing stables, Liselle, Maud, and the remaining onlookers watched in terror. Then, above the sound of the flames, they could hear the clatter of hooves inside the stables, which was followed by a horse and rider leaping over the flaming barricade, closely followed by the other two. The three riders brought their terrified steeds to a halt with considerable difficulty, but eventually managed to slide from their backs. The first soldier's faced was blackened from smoke and his clothes were singed. Again, he shouted orders and very quickly, a line formed between the inn and a water pump on the other side of the street. Soon, buckets of water passed swiftly along the chain of soldiers towards the burning building. Liselle found herself in the middle of a second line, which was returning the empty buckets to the pump. More soldiers were arriving from other parts of the town, other lines were forming up, and in next to no time, the flames began to die down.

As Liselle was passing a used bucket back down the line, she felt a firm push in the small of her back, which sent her sprawling headlong onto the dirty street. As quick hands helped her to her feet, she turned round to face her assailant and found herself looking straight into the long face of the horse that she had ridden the day before.

The she turned to look at the man who had helped her up, and saw that he was the soldier that had been shouting orders and not the horse's owner as she had expected. Gratefully, she thanked the man, who stared back at her blankly.

"Well then?" said the dirty faced soldier.

"Well then what?" asked Liselle indignantly. After all, she had thanked him, and hadn't really required his help to stand up.

"What do you mean, well then what? It snowed, didn't it? Don't tell me you didn't try it out."

Liselle stared at the man in total bewilderment.

"Please tell me you tried the sledge," said Charlie.

Chapter 7
Culapium

Joe walked for several hours before stopping by the wayside for a rest. He had passed few people on the road and those that he had were all travelling in the opposite direction. Most were sad faced refugees, displaced by the war and seeking a new place to live. Their few possessions, hastily thrown together, were stacked on horse drawn carts, or were carried by pack mules.

Joe sat at the base of a large tree whose roots spread across the dirt road, causing deep ruts that would catch out an unwary traveller. He rested his back against the trunk of the tree and opened his pack. He took out one of the bread rolls and breaking off a chunk, he ate it hungrily. Joe pulled off another piece and eating more slowly he leaned his head back against the tree. It was only then that he noticed that he had company. Directly in front of him sitting in the middle of the rutted road was a dog. There was nothing special about the animal, it was a typical mongrel, but it stared intently at Joe. Its piercing eyes and tight-lipped mouth made Joe feel uneasy.

"Go away," shouted Joe, hurling a stone at the dog.

The dog moved its head slightly to one side and the stone flew harmlessly into the hedge on the other side of the road. It watched Joe eagerly.

"Stupid mutt. I don't have enough spare to go giving good food to mangy old dogs. And you're not going to eat me either."

Joe finished the roll he was eating and pulled an apple from the bag. As he took a bite, the dog barked at him and shuffled forward a few inches.

"All right, you can have the core when I've finished."

The dog barked again and lay down, apparently satisfied.

When Joe had finished most of the apple, true to his word, he threw the remainder to the dog. His aim was wildly inaccurate, but the dog moved instantly and leaped silently, plucking the apple core from the air with ease. It sat back down and biting the core in two, swallowed twice. It looked thankfully at Joe and barked once.

"My pleasure," said Joe smiling. He stood up, shouldered his pack, and walked towards the dog.

"You're quite a good boy really, aren't you?" he said reaching out his hand to stroke the dog's head.

The dog stepped back out of reach and sat down again, looking at Joe with the same intense stare.

"Suit you then," shrugged Joe. "I'm off now anyway."

He turned his back on the dog and resumed his journey along the road.

Presently he noticed movement at the corner of his eye. Trotting silently along, on the other side of the road, was the dog. Joe pretended not to notice and eased up his pace. The dog also slowed, keeping parallel with him. Then Joe broke into a run, and instantly the dog followed suit. They trotted on together for a couple of miles until finally Joe ran out of breath and had to stop. Puffing hard and leaning heavily with his hands on his knees, he looked at the dog. The dog sat quite still, in turn observing Joe. It wasn't panting and hadn't even broken into a sweat.

"Alright then dog, you can come with me," said Joe, once he had regained his breath. Joe wasn't sure that he had much choice in the matter anyway.

The dog barked once, and cocked its head comically to one side. Joe felt sure that the dog was laughing at him.

As they followed the road, Joe found that he was happy to have the company, and chatted amiably to the dog, explaining to him where they were headed. Joe had decided that the dog was male, but couldn't be completely sure, unable as he was to get near to the animal. The dog, for his own part, appeared to listen intently to Joe's narrative, pricking up his ears as Joe told him of their lucky escape from the monastery. Joe glossed over the part of his story about the dragons. He was not concerned that the dog would tell anyone, but he did worry about who might hear him. If the dog had noticed that there was a large gap in Joe's tale then he didn't let on.

A peculiarity of the dog's that Joe noticed, was that he would hide whenever they passed any other travellers on the road. Long before Joe could see or hear anyone coming, the dog would stop and listen alertly, before bounding behind the nearest trees or disappearing round a hedge. Joe would continue walking and presently, after the refugees or soldiers had passed, the dog would come loping up. Joe couldn't think of any real reason for the dog's strange behaviour, other than, whilst clearly very intelligent, he was probably quite a shy creature. After all, the dog wouldn't allow Joe to come near him either.

As nightfall approached, Joe started to look out for some shelter for the night. Despite his misgivings about Liselle's idea of breaking into people's homes, he didn't particularly fancy the idea of sleeping out in the rough. It wasn't long before they found a small hamlet set a couple of hundred yards back from the road, and having made certain that all of the buildings were empty, Joe found an unlooked door, and he and his new companion settled down for the night.

Joe slept well, dreaming contentedly of Daniel and Liselle, and the dragons. They were all soaring high above the clouds, occasionally diving down through the gaps, and then burst up through the clouds into the bright sunshine.

Joe awoke late, the sun already high in the sky. He looked round for the dog, but could not see him in the room. Rising hastily, Joe searched the other two rooms in the house, but his new friend was not in the building. Dejectedly, Joe sat down at the kitchen table and ate a meagre breakfast, as he did not feel much like eating. He thought about Daniel and Liselle, and hoped that his friends were safe.

He was contemplating how the dog had managed to open the door to get out when an odd noise at the door made him jump. Quickly, Joe slipped beneath the table and started to focus his mind in readiness for releasing the Repulsion Charm. The strange noise stopped, and then Joe watched fearfully as the latch on the door slowly began to rise.

He continued to mutter the first part of the charm as the door opened, only to reveal the dog upright on his hind feet pushing the door. Joe let out a huge sigh of relief and relaxed carefully so as not to release the charm. The dog, having opened the door fully, dropped to the ground and looked at Joe quizzically.

Joe climbed back out from under the table. "You're back then," he said to his faithful companion.

The dog turned around, put his forepaws onto the door, and pushed it shut, which explained the odd sound that Joe had heard. Then he nosed the latch back into place, before finally turning around to look at Joe with a distinctly proud appearance.

"Very clever," said Joe, impressed, but also feeling somewhat foolish. "Well, I won't ask where you've been, but I hope you found something to eat, because this bag isn't bottomless, you know?"

The dog barked once, and regretfully, Joe reached into the bag and walking round the table, he gave the dog a piece of salted meat.

They continued eastwards, following the same road. The further they went the fewer people they saw. As dusk approached, a large cavalry troupe overtook them, and true to form, the dog disappeared from sight, only this time he did not reappear.

As Joe entered the next deserted village, a scruffy man stepped out from behind one of the abandoned houses. Joe took an instant dislike to the man, who was dishonest looking and addressed him in a gruff manner. With one eye on Joe's pack, the man suggested that they look for a place together, as they would be safer in numbers. Joe declined politely but firmly, and continued through the village. The man shrugged and walked away, in the opposite direction. Joe found a small insignificant looking house on the far side of the village, and settled down for the night. He fell asleep, listening to the sound of light rain falling on the roof.

Joe awoke suddenly; he had heard a strange noise. It was still dark and there was the unmistakable smell of wet dog. Joe's companion had rejoined him at some point during the night. Joe started to relax, but as his eyes grew accustomed to the dark, he could see that the front door was open. Glancing around the room, he saw only the dog, which was staring intently at the door to the next room. Seeing nothing suspicious, Joe approached the door, and focusing his mind, he uttered the words of the Repelling Charm and the door swung shut.

"That's a rare talent you have there young man," said a gruff sounding voice.

Joe spun around, dropping low and facing the direction of the voice. Out of the shadows in the corner came the shifty looking man from earlier. The long knife in the man's hand was enough to convince Joe that his early assessment had been correct, and he was glad that he had not joined the man when asked.

"The charm works just as well on thieves and murderers," said Joe bravely.

"Let's test that theory of yours, shall we?" sneered the man, leaping forward with surprising speed.

Before Joe could react, the dog jumped at the assailant biting deeply into his arm. Screaming in agony, the man dropped his knife. He pulled away his injured arm, and fled through the open door into the night.

The following day, Joe arrived at the hospital town of Culapium and soon found his mother at the main hospital, where she was on duty in one of the wards. Surprised but overjoyed to see her son, Joe's mother was quick to ask for an explanation.

"I'm glad I didn't hear about it," she said, when Joe told her about the attack on the monastery.

"That's why I wanted to come and tell you," explained Joe.

As she was still on duty, Joe's mother gave him directions to the house where she lived. Joe was about to leave, when he noticed a man lying in a bed at the far end of the ward.

"Who's that man over there?" asked Joe, pointing towards the patient, who was nursing a bandaged arm.

"He's somebody you don't want to know," answered Joe's mother severely. Her mouth tightened as she spoke and she frowned. "His name's Regan and he's a rather nasty individual. There are some strange things going on around here," she whispered to her son. "Most of the soldiers, those that are well enough, have moved off to the front lines. So there's nobody really left to police the town, and men like that one are taking advantage of the situation."

She explained how gangs had moved in swiftly and were taking over control of the town. They spread rumours about how Koronian spies had infiltrated every element of the town, and only they, the gangs, would be able to protect the townsfolk. Of course, the gangs would provide protection, but at a price.

Joe's mother nodded her head towards the injured man. "He's in one of the larger gangs, and was brought in by his friends last night. He claimed that he had been attacked by a wolf. Certainly, his injuries were awful, but I think it is more likely that they had been caused by a large dog. I've never heard of any wolves in this part of the country, so I think his tall story is yet another way of scaring people into parting with their money."

"You're right; he was bitten by my dog when he tried to rob us last night," said Joe.

"That doesn't surprise me," said Joe's mother. "You weren't hurt were you?"

"No, I'm fine," answered Joe.

"Since when did you have a dog?" asked his mother, looking around. "I didn't think the orphanage allowed that sort of thing."

"He's not mine really; sometimes it feels more like the other way round. We met on the road a couple of days together, and travelled here together. He's really very clever; you'll see when you meet him."

"You haven't brought him into the hospital, have you?"

"No, of course I haven't. Actually, I don't know where he is, but that isn't unusual. I don't think he likes people very much."

"Certainly not that one," said Joe's mother, looking again at the man with the bandaged arm.

Joe also looked at the man, who happened to look their way and his eyes opened wide in recognition. Immediately, he turned to the man at his bedside and started talking quickly.

"I think it's time for you to go Joe," said Joe's mother.

"I was beginning to think the same," said Joe.

"Here, take my door key and let yourself in. Can you remember the directions I gave you?"

"Yes, I think so, I'll see you later," replied Joe, moving rapidly towards the doorway; the gang member was already crossing the ward towards Joe.

As soon as Joe was outside, he sprinted across the road and disappeared up a narrow alleyway. He didn't slow until he had made a few more turnings and could be sure that the man wasn't following. Pausing briefly to regain his breath, Joe realised that he was now well and truly lost. The town was not large, but it was big enough, with plenty of narrow alleys for someone unfamiliar with the place to lose himself. Remembering the name of the district where his mother lived, Joe asked a passer by for directions, and was soon on the right track. Once he had reached the right area of town, Joe recalled enough of what his mother had told him to reach the street where she lived.

As Joe approached the house that his mother had described to him, he saw a familiar form sitting in front of the door.

"That's impossible," said Joe to the dog. "There's no way that you could have known where my mother lived."

He looked at the dog suspiciously. "You are not a normal animal," he said accusingly.

The dog cocked his head to one side and looked at Joe in the same way he always did when Joe talked to him.

"And I'm sure you understand every word I say."

Later that day, Joe's mother returned home. The dog did not seem to mind her, and she was happy for him to stay.

"I don't think you should return to the hospital Joe. Regan asked me lots of questions after you'd left. I told him you were an old patient and wouldn't be in town for long. I said I didn't know where you were staying and didn't expect to see you again. I think he believed me, but we should be careful. Clearly he harbours a grudge after what your dog did to him."

Joe's mother explained that she would discharge Regan in the morning, so that would be an end to any trouble. Joe however was not so optimistic.

The next morning, accompanied by the dog, discretely he followed his mother to work. He thought it strange that the dog was no longer shying away from people, but said nothing. Hidden in the shadows of an alleyway, they watched the front door of the hospital. They did not have to wait long before they saw a man with a bandaged arm leaving the building.

Joe and the dog followed Regan across town to a large mansion house situated in a nice relatively unspoilt neighbourhood. Watching from a safe distance, Joe could see more gang members around the house. He watched for a while as they came and went, evidently carrying money and often accompanied by the sound of callous laughter.

Back home that evening, Joe told his mother what he had seen. After reprimanding him for taking risks, she explained that the old house had belonged previously to a sweet old lady, who had passed away unexpectedly. Almost immediately, the gang had moved in, with one of their members claiming to be her nephew. Nobody believed him, but then nobody was willing to confront the gang. They had been there ever since, and used the place as a base from which to conduct their crimes.

After promising not to get involved in anything foolish, Joe helped his mother to prepare dinner.

"You're quite at home in the kitchen," observed Joe's mother, as he peeled their potatoes.

Joe laughed and told her all about the sledging incident, and the subsequent punishment.

She laughed out loud, and then said gently, "I looked in on you last night while you were asleep. For someone who has experience so much recently, you sleep very well Joe. What do you dream about?"

"I don't know, I never remember my dreams," Joe lied, concentrating on the vegetables.

"That's a pity, because you appear to enjoy them; you looked very contented."

Chapter 8
Into the East

Daniel had been travelling over the rough terrain for about two hours when a large group of well-armed men surprised and surrounded him. Appearing as if from nowhere, the men rose from the long grasses and, encircling him, they cut off any chance he might have of escape. They did not look friendly and their leather clothes, bearskin boots, and fur hats identified them clearly as a Koronian raiding party. Daniel had never seen a Koronian before, but the monks at the monastery had described them well enough and there was no doubting where this group were from.

Fortunately, for Daniel, the raiding party had completed their mission of disruption and had started their journey back across the plains to the East. If they had still had work to do then Daniel would have been killed instantly, rather than risk having him alert anyone to their presence. So instead, after relieving him of his pack, they took him with them.

None of the Koronians spoke his language, but it was not difficult to understand their hand gestures and the shoves in his back propelled him in the right direction. Swiftly, they moved towards the border and did not stop to rest until one of the watch towers came into sight. Shrinking down into the tall grass, the party lay low and did not move. Exhausted, Daniel soon fell asleep.

He was woken by a sharp jab in his ribs. A hand clasped firmly over his mouth smothered his cry of alarm. It felt to Daniel like he had only just fallen asleep, but it was already dark and he felt cold and hungry. As though they had read his mind, one of the Koronians gave him a piece of dry meat. Then the man gave Daniel some water, followed by a mouthful of a bitter tasting drink that made his throat burn. No sooner had he finished his meagre meal than he was hauled to his feet and they were off again. The food warmed him, the strange drink made him light headed, and his aching legs did not hurt as much. They had waited until nightfall before attempting to cross the border, which would have been in full view of the watchtowers in daylight. Daniel was amazed at how easily the Koronians passed back into their own territory completely unhindered. Any attempt to cross in daylight would have been met with swift action. A signal passed from a watchtower by mirror, flame or smoke to one of the forts would have brought forth a large cavalry charge. In no time at all heavy horses would have borne down on them, but at nighttime they passed by unseen.

The pace was relentless and they continued until the steel cold dawn caused Daniel to shiver frequently. The food and drink had long worn off and his legs felt numb as he stumbled along. They had already encountered other Koronian scouting patrols that, following a short challenge, allowed them to pass. Finally, when they reached a large forest far inside Koronian territory, they stopped briefly to rest. Daniel was given some more food and another shot of the bitter drink.

Daniel lay back on the forest floor and stared up into the canopy overhead, listening to the birds calling to one another. He breathed deeply and the smell of summer filled his lungs as he pondered his situation. This was precisely the direction that Daniel had wanted to travel, but he hadn't anticipated it to be in this manner. His idea had been to sneak across the border, steal some clothes, and then seek out the other orphans. He could see now that his plan had been useless from the start. There was no way that he would have managed to get past the numerous patrols and of course, he could not understand a word of the Koronians complicated sounding language. He knew what Liselle and Joe would say to him. They would not have done anything as foolhardy as he had done.

As Daniel dwelt on his predicament, a thought occurred to him. He could use the Translation Charm. At least he would if he could remember it properly, and if he had been any good at Charms. He thought of his friends, especially Joe, who could have done it easily. Daniel was beginning to feel very alone.

Pulled once more to his feet, Daniel was guided into the forest. They no longer ran but walked briskly through the trees, following well-worn narrow paths that wound around ancient trees. Around midday, they arrived at a large military camp. A solid wooden stockade surrounded the wooden buildings housed within.

Daniel was handed over to a weasel-looking man, who at least spoke his language. The man showed no interest in Daniel other than to escort him to a roughly made billet, where four men were making ready to depart the camp. The group consisted of a tall soldier, a pleasant looking one who was in charge, a rather severe looking man and fourth, who just looked like he would rather be somewhere else. They were not impressed with the idea of taking Daniel with them, but had little choice. The weasel-faced man told Daniel that the men would take him on to the next place, but gave no more information than that. They gave Daniel time to eat a quick meal, and then left the camp by a small gate.

Over the next two days, Daniel repeatedly practised the Translation Charm. To begin with, he was able to pick up the odd word and then he would have to repeat the charm every time his concentration wavered. In time, he remembered the charm more precisely and his concentration improved as he relaxed. By the end of the second day, he could understand the gist of what the Koronians were talking about and with a single incantation, he could sustain the charm for about an hour if his concentration was uninterrupted.

They did not move as quickly as the raiding party had, but Daniel still struggled to keep up with the men. They stopped for one of their regular breaks.

"Here, have some more," said the tall soldier offering Daniel a bottle of the drink that his captors were so fond of. He had been plying Daniel with the drink regularly, each time they rested.

Daniel drank it swiftly; he was acquiring a taste for the bitter drink. He tried to return the bottle, and stumbled. He was unable to prevent himself from giggling childishly.

"I told you not to give him too much," said the kind soldier.

The quiet soldier suddenly spoke, quite surprising his fellow men at arms.

"You know he's listening to us, don't you? He understands what we're saying," he said, gesturing towards Daniel, who had sat down and recanted the Translation Charm.

"Why does he keep muttering like that?" asked the tall soldier.

"It's their silly magic," sneered the cruel looking soldier. "It's nothing compared to ours. All they do is mutter their little charms. It doesn't come close to the fireballs our mages can conjure up."

"What about translocation?" suggested the quiet man.

"It's a myth, completely impossible. I've never seen anybody do it, and I'd just as soon believe in dragons as believe in translocation."

"You never believe in anything."

"I'm a practical man. I understand only what I can see."

Daniel thought about Brother Bart's translocation and his ride on the dragon, and shaking his head, he smiled to himself at the soldier's ignorance.

"Somebody disagrees with you," said the friendly soldier, pointing a half-eaten drumstick at Daniel.

"He really is listening to us then," said the tall soldier. "That's very clever."

Daniel couldn't help but smile again as the drink relaxed his self-control. It did not go unnoticed by the nasty soldier.

"Well hear this child. Where you're going, they'll soon wipe that arrogant smirk off your face. I doubt if you'll last more then a week in the slave mines. I've seen big men go in there only to be dragged out a month later wishing they were dead. You mark my words, if you really can understand us, then you've nothing to smile about."

Suddenly Daniel didn't feel so clever. Until then, the Koronians had treated him well and Daniel had even grown to like some of them, especially the leader. He glared at the nasty soldier, who grinned evilly at him.

"Leave him alone," said the kind soldier. "It'll be bad enough for him without you making him feel worse."

The nasty one sneered and turned away.

The nice soldier then turned to Daniel and spoke to him. He explained that most of them wanted to see an end to the war, which would also see an end to the slave labour. That was something else that he did not agree with.

"Here's one word of advice for you. Don't let them know that you can understand our language. They may think you're a spy and you don't want to know what happens to spies."

Later that afternoon they arrived at the mines. It was not an inviting place. They stood on the edge of a large quarry. The sides were sheer and there was only one narrow path by which to descend. Leaving the others at the top, the kind soldier escorted Daniel to one of the many huts that were scattered around the floor of the quarry.

Inside the hut sat a burly guard, who leered at Daniel as they entered. Without saying a word, the guard reached into a box behind him, and produced a leather collar. He fitted it around Daniel's neck, marking him as a slave. It was clasped at the back and was not unlike those Daniel had seen on dogs. It hung loosely round his neck, but the guard did not seem bothered. The guard grunted and sat back down.

The kind soldier led him from the hut, and they walked towards a large rock face. Neither of them spoke. Daniel fiddled nervously with his new collar, and looked about him. Men with collars fitted worked with saws and axes, cutting wood into planks and posts. Small groups of guards milled around, chatting casually to one another. Daniel and the soldier reached the rock face, where there were three entrances carved into the stone. Slaves passed to and from the tunnels behind carrying heavy sacks.

At the entrance, one of the guards thrust an axe towards Daniel. Daniel took the axe, but nearly dropped it; it was so heavy. Heaving it onto his shoulder, he trudged after the man who led them down a steep mineshaft. Daniel could see where timber shored up the shaft using the posts as uprights and the planks as the ceiling.

More than once, Daniel slipped and fell, bruising his knees and scraping his arms on the walls as he tried to steady himself. They arrived quickly at a dimly lit room of sorts, where another burly guard was sitting at a makeshift desk. It was here that the kind soldier was to hand over Daniel, but he tried to convince the guard otherwise.

"He's too young, I'm telling you. Look at his puny arms. He can barely lift that axe, let alone wield it properly," the soldier explained to the guard.

"That's not my problem. Anyway, he doesn't have to *wield* the axe. It's not a sword. All he has to do is to scrape at the rock to begin with and after two or three years I'm sure his arms will be strong enough to use it properly."

"You know he shouldn't be here. He should be down at Thraldom working in the kitchens or something. Look at his collar, even that doesn't fit him."

"So I'll put an extra hole in it to tighten it. Let's hope I remember to take it off his neck when I punch the new hole," he grinned maliciously.

The soldier gave up and turned to Daniel.

"Good luck lad," said the soldier sadly. "Here's one word of advice for you. Keep your head down and stay out of trouble."

"Why are you talking to him? They're too stupid to understand us," said the guard ignorantly.

"Of course they are," said the soldier winking slyly at Daniel.

Daniel was sad to see the kind soldier go as he watched him head back up the shaft. However, the emotion was soon replaced by fear as the surly guard grabbed Daniel by the collar hanging loosely about his neck. Forcefully he removed the collar and used the sharp point of Daniel's axe to put an extra hole in the leather, before tightening it roughly back round Daniel's neck. Daniel choked and tried to put his finger through the collar to pull it away from his throat.

The guard snatched Daniel's hand back down.

"Leave it alone," he growled. "Nice and tight is it now?" he sneered. "Don't ever think about taking it off, or you'll never see daylight again."

As tears welled in Daniel's eyes, the guard pushed the axe into his hands and dragged him along the next passageway. Flaming torches in sconces positioned regularly along the walls lit the route. Daniel coughed as the smoke reached his lungs.

"You'll get used to it," muttered the guard, "not that you can understand me."

He laughed to himself then stopped and looked at Daniel.

"You don't know what I'm saying do you?" he eyed Daniel suspiciously.

Daniel stared blankly back at the guard.

"No I thought not," said the guard seemingly satisfied. "You're all like dumb animals to me."

Shortly they arrived at a junction with three other passages that branched off in different directions and at different angles. The guard stopped briefly, and then pulled Daniel up a passage that sloped steeply upwards. It quickly opened out into a small chamber where half a dozen slaves were working at a rock face. Two guards lounged by the entrance. The burly guard talked briefly to them, and then pushed Daniel over to the rock, in a space between two other slaves.

Daniel hacked at the rock, and tossed the loose stone on a pile behind him. The burly guard watched for a short while, then grunted and left the chamber.

"Hey, you," whispered the man next to Daniel.

Daniel stopped working and turned towards the man who was talking to him.

"No, don't stop," hissed the man, glancing nervously over his shoulder at the guards.

Daniel immediately returned to hacking at the rock face with his pickaxe.

"Sorry, I didn't mean to startle you," said the man, continuing with his own work. "But you need to keep working. We're allowed to talk quietly, but we mustn't ever stop digging."

"Right, thanks," responded Daniel, smiling.

The man smiled back.

"I couldn't help noticing earlier, but were you listening to the guards?"

Daniel eyed the man suspiciously.

"I thought so," said the man. "You were using the Translation Charm, weren't you? It's alright; sometimes I use it as well," he added quickly, noticing the look on Daniel's face. "Ever since I was a child, I've been quite good at Protective Charms, but it wasn't until I was brought here that I found a use for them."

Daniel nodded his understanding.

"What's your name?" asked the man.

Daniel told him.

"Hello Daniel, my name's Will and I think that we're going to get on just fine."

Daniel didn't say it but he agreed. There was something very likeable about his new friend and also something a bit familiar.

After a considerable time spent chipping away at the rock, the slave workers were allowed to rest for a short time. When none of the guards was looking, Daniel used the Healing Charm on the blisters that covered his hands and on the injuries that he had incurred during his descent earlier that morning.

Carefully Will, who had been watching, leaned over towards Daniel. "I never did learn that one. Do you think that you could teach me?" he asked in a whisper.

Daniel nodded.

That evening, after they had been shepherded to one of the huts back on the surface, Daniel recanted the Healing Charm to Will who immediately started to practise on his own sores. Seeing what Daniel was doing, some of the other slave workers approached him cautiously. He did what he could for their injuries, some of which were very old. Many of the other slave workers coughed badly. Daniel tried to ease their pain, but no amount of healing could remove the smoke and dust from their lungs.

Daniel slept soundly, both from the day's hard work, and because he knew sleep would bring the usual dreams. He dreamt of his friends, Liselle and Joe, and the green dragon. They were all flying together, playing a game of chase around snow-capped mountaintops. The green, red, and gold dragons turned effortlessly around the craggy spires as they attempted to escape.

The following morning the men with bad coughs that he had helped the night before seemed to be coughing worse than ever. Daniel was concerned that they would blame him, but he had only been trying to help. He need not have worried. The men thanked him, explaining that even though they were coughing badly, they could breathe more easily than they had done for years and asked Daniel if he could try again that evening.

At the end of another day in the mines, the more grateful men even shared their bread ration with Daniel. He took it gratefully; after a day's work and an evening of healing, he was ravenous.

"He's a growing lad," observed one man.

"Exactly," said another. "He shouldn't even be here, he's far too young."

"Lucky for us that he is though," said another selfishly.

"I didn't see you share any of your bread with him after he healed your bad leg," criticised the first man.

The selfish man looked sheepish and scuttled off to a far corner of the hut.

The days were long and they toiled endlessly. Each morning they were woken at dawn and herded like animals to the mine entrances. After an hour's work, they were allowed a brief rest to eat a meagre breakfast of bread and water. They didn't stop then until the day's end, when at sunset they returned to the huts. They were provided with water to wash themselves, followed by a supper of bread and stew, the contents of which were unrecognisable and tasted awful.

"Tastes like chicken," said one man.

"I swear, if you say that one more time, you're a dead man," said the selfish man savagely from his corner.

According to Will, the man had been repeating the same line every night since his arrival eight months earlier. Most had become used to his little joke and a few laughed every time. The man had admitted once that he was going to stop saying it, but then he realised how much it annoyed the selfish man, so kept going.

At the end of each day, they filed along the mineshafts to appear at the surface, blinking their eyes against the bright but fading daylight. Daniel spent the evenings healing or teaching the Healing Charm, for which the other men were very grateful. After a particularly difficult day and long evening, even the selfish man with the bad leg gave Daniel some of his water.

"Thanks," said Daniel gratefully.

The man smiled, for probably the first time in years.

One day, Daniel broached the subject of escape with Will. As they worked, he whispered quietly to Will, between the chipping noises of their axes.

"There are loads of us. We outnumber the guards here easily," he said.

"Sure, we could take them any time that we wanted. Then what would we do? The forest is crawling with Koronians and we are miles from home. We'd achieve nothing by it."

Deflated, Daniel had to agree, but he refused to consider the possibility that he would be spending the rest of his life as a slave.

"What do you dream about?" asked Will suddenly. "Sorry I don't mean to be rude, but most men here have nightmares. You appear to sleep soundly and sometimes you look like you're smiling."

"Oh, I don't know," lied Daniel, "I'm probably thinking about being home."

Quickly Daniel changed the subject.

"We've been together for some time now and I've noticed that you never talk about your past."

"No I don't generally," responded Will quietly. "It's quite a painful subject for me."

"I'm sorry. I didn't mean to upset you."

"That's alright. I don't think you could. I should probably talk about how things were before, otherwise I might forget.

"I dream of one day being reunited with my wife and son. I haven't seen them for such a long time. My wife worked as a nurse for the army and my son would be about the same age as you."

"What's his name?" asked Daniel.

"Joe," replied Will simply.

Chapter 9
Soldiers and Officers

Finally, Liselle recognised the man for the brother he was. She flung her arms around him and squeezed tightly.

"I haven't seen you for more than a year and you want to talk about that sledge," she said accusingly, looking up at Charlie.

"Come on, you did promise to tell me. Don't you remember?"

"Yes, of course I do, and we did try it out. The abbot caught us as well."

"That was inevitable. So are you going to tell all or am I going to die of old age waiting for you."

While Liselle told her sledging story, they continued to help put out the fire, which did not take long. Charlie was pleased to hear that his creation had been such a success.

With the fire out, the soldiers that had helped began to disperse, and one of them led poor Maud away from the smouldering ruins of her home. Charlie asked Liselle how she had come to be inside a burning inn, but before she was able to reply, a stern sounding voice interrupted them.

"Ah Sergeant, there you are," said the voice firmly.

Charlie snapped to attention. Liselle looked towards the source of the voice and saw a small round man in uniform walking towards them. Evidently, the man was an officer, and Liselle understood her brother's reaction to his voice.

"I've been looking for you, young man," said the officer.

"Yes sir, there was a fire," Charlie started to explain.

"Oh yes, yes, I know all about that," said the officer shortly. "What I want to know now is how it started and how you managed to get it under control so quickly."

Charlie explained that he suspected arson on the part of the Koronians, maybe through a spy, as it was extremely unlikely that Maud would have gone to bed leaving a naked flame burning anywhere in the inn. In addition, he suspected that the fire had started in the stables, which was a good source of flammable material such as hay.

"And what about putting out the fire; who achieved that?" asked the officer directly.

"Well sir," Charlie stuttered, "I suppose everybody had a hand in it; we all worked together."

"Nonsense," retorted the officer. "I know full well that you rallied everybody, and I feel totally justified in having promoted you."

"Thank you sir, but we didn't save the building. It's beyond repair."

"Yes, but at least the fire didn't spread. That's the main thing," said the officer. "You did an excellent job here Sergeant."

"Thank you sir," replied Charlie snappily. "Although I did have some assistance," he added, gesturing towards the Liselle and others that had lingered behind.

"Of course, of course," said the officer, beaming proudly at the rest of the soldiers. "Well done everybody. An excellent job! I think that a good night's rest is required, what is left of it, anyway."

Dawn was breaking, so the officer dismissed the soldiers, advising that light duties would be the order of the day for everyone. As the men slipped away, the officer turned his attention back to Charlie.

"Now then Sergeant, are you going to introduce me to this young lady. She looks remarkably like you; don't tell me she's your young sister that we've all heard so much about."

Liselle's face would have turned bright red if it had not been so dirty from the smoke and soot. She never imagined that Charlie would have talked about her, especially to his commanding officer.

Charlie introduced Liselle to the officer whose name was Colonel Potts. The colonel shook Liselle's hand warmly, and then looked at the inn.

"I guess you won't be staying there again," he murmured sadly, shaking his head. "Right, follow me, you two."

They followed Colonel Potts as he strode down the street.

"He's a good man," said Joe quietly. "Not always the brightest and he's certainly not as young as he once was, but we do well by him. He looks after us and gives credit where it's due."

"Speaking of credit where it's due," said Liselle looking at the stripes on her brother's arm. "When were you promoted to Sergeant?"

"It was only last week. I wrote and told you, but I don't think that you'll be receiving that letter any time soon."

Liselle looked up at her brother as they walked through the quiet night.

"Our parents would have been very proud of you," she said softly and put her hand in his. Charlie squeezed her hand tightly and they walked on together.

Liselle explained about the attack on the monastery. "There's nothing for me to go back to. Can I stay here with you? I can help, I'll do anything," she asked.

"We'll have to ask the Colonel. I can't make that kind of decision. There are many soldiers in this town and he may think that you'll just be in the way. So don't go getting your hopes up alright."

"Of course she can stay," said Colonel Potts when they asked him later in his office. The Colonel beamed at them from behind his untidy desk. "We need every man and woman willing to help. I wish that there were more like you young lady," he said to the delighted Liselle, who grinned back at the old man.

"In fact, I could do with some help in my office. Just look at this mess," he said gesturing towards the piles of papers heaped all over his desk. "I assume that you can read and write."

Liselle nodded enthusiastically.

"And of course, you'll need somewhere to stay. We can't have you sleeping in the barracks. How would you like temporary accommodation with Mrs Potts and me?

Our boys are long grown up and it would be nice to have a fresh face around the house again. What do you think, could you put up with a couple of doddery old codgers?"

Speechless, Liselle glanced at her brother who looked back at her encouragingly.

"I think I would like that very much," she said to the colonel.

"Good, then it's all arranged. Your brother can even come round every evening to see you."

Charlie shuffled his feet and appeared uncomfortable.

"Erm, thank you sir, but I'm not sure about," he trailed off quietly.

"What? Oh right I see what you mean. No, you're quite right Sergeant. How would it look if you were coming to my house every evening? After all, what would the men say? We can't have favouritism and all that. Well, I'm sure that we can arrange something."

Charlie relaxed and stood up straight. "Thank you sir," he said with evident relief.

Liselle spent the next few days working for the Colonel. She helped him to tidy his office and put all of his records in order, and occasionally ran small errands. They consisted for the most part of passing on messages, either by word or by notes hastily scrawled on odd scraps of paper. Liselle enjoyed her work and she would often see her brother during the course of the day.

Mrs Potts had greeted Liselle as if she was a long lost daughter and they immediately became firm friends. Liselle was put up in the youngest son's room, which looked out over the little garden at the back of the colonel's modest home.

After work, Liselle and the Colonel walked home to be met by a hearty meal prepared by the ever-busy Mrs Potts. In the evening, Liselle would seek out Charlie and they would walk around the town, talking about anything and everything. Often they talked about the monastery. Although Charlie hadn't enjoyed his time there very much, he was deeply upset by the news of the monk's deaths and the capture of the other children.

Liselle, for her own part, was fascinated by the war. She would listen intently to the colonel's conversations, a fact that had not gone unnoticed by Colonel Potts, usually resulting in her being sent out of the office on seemingly pointless errands. Liselle would question her brother about what she had heard, and he was always willing to answer questions.

"What did the colonel mean by the major offensive?" Liselle asked her brother as they sat under a large tree one hot evening.

"There's going to be a big push," replied Charlie quietly. "Everybody will be involved; we're not leaving anyone behind. Finally, we should be able to end this war."

"Isn't that a bit risky?" asked Liselle. "I mean, committing the entire army sounds very dangerous to me. What if something went wrong?"

"Nothing can go wrong. We'll have the protection of the monks. I didn't tell you this before, but one of the reasons that the monastery became an orphanage was because most of the monks have been training in secret places across the land."

That evening, Liselle returned to the colonel's house with her head swimming with thoughts. She joined Mrs Potts in the front room, where they sat quietly.

"What do you dream about when you're asleep my dear?" Mrs Potts asked tenderly.

"Oh, I don't know, lots of things I suppose," said Liselle lying. "Why do you ask?"

"Well, when I've looked in on you in the morning to see if you're awake, you always have such a lovely smile on your face. I was sure you must be dreaming about something wonderful."

Liselle shrugged her shoulders and smiled.

Chapter 10
Fire Magic

Liselle felt herself shaken roughly and there were shouts of, "Fire." For an instant, Liselle imagined that she was back in the burning Inn. She discovered that the truth was worse still; this time the whole town was under attack. The colonel's wife explained quickly that they had to dress and leave as soon as possible; the Koronians were using fire magic in their attack and most of the town was already ablaze. Hastily, Liselle leapt from her bed and threw on some clothes.

"I didn't think I was going to be able to wake you. Maud told me that you were a deep sleeper, but I never thought…well it doesn't matter now. You're awake and we still have the chance to escape."

"What do you mean, escape?" asked Liselle worriedly. "Can't we put out the fires and fight back?"

"Not this time my dear, I'm sorry to say," answered Mrs Potts, rushing down the stairs.

"Where are we going?" called out Liselle, as she followed the colonel's wife out into the street.

Mrs Potts did not reply, as the scene that met them as they left the building filled both of them with terror. It appeared almost as if every building in the town was burning. The heat from the flames emanating from the building opposite hit them full in the face, and they gasped desperately for air. Mrs Potts gripped Liselle's hand tightly and pulled her down a small side street. The air was cooler and they were soon able to breathe more easily.

"That was close," said Liselle, drawing deep breaths.

"We're not safe yet," said Mrs Potts seriously. "Come on, this way."

As they ran, the colonel's wife shouted over the noise of the burning, explaining to Liselle what had happened.

"Your young Charlie came to the house a short while ago to warn us of the attack. He said the Koronians had taken them completely by surprise, unleashing a barrage of fireballs on the East Gate, destroying it. The colonel and I were awoken by the noise; how you slept through it, I'll never know. Anyway, Charlie burst through our front door, nearly knocking over Colonel Potts who was on his way out. Charlie said we should rendezvous at the West Gate."

"Where's the colonel?" yelled Liselle.

"He left with Charlie. Oh, I do hope they'll be all right. We've suffered some attacks before and survived them, but they've never been like this before."

They ran on down the alleyway, glad to be away from the intense heat of the fire. As they turned into the next street, it however contained as big a problem as the first; smoke filled the street and they had to cover their mouths with their clothes. Running on blindly, they ran down the smoke-heavy road until, coughing badly, they found fresh air again in the following street. Their eyes stung and they blinked quickly, as they looked around to get their bearings.

"Do you know where we are?" wheezed Liselle.

"Yes, I think so," replied Mrs Potts, when her breath had returned. "We're not far now from the West Gate. It's only a couple of streets away and there don't appear to be any buildings burning between the gate and us. Let's walk slowly for now."

Liselle agreed readily, and took the opportunity to glance back over her shoulder. Above the glowing red of the town, thick black smoke raced skyward, accompanied occasionally by large fireballs, from either burning buildings or the Koronians fire magic. Liselle looked at Mrs Potts, who did not appear well; she was panting heavily and her face and clothes were covered with black from the fire and smoke. Liselle assumed that she must look the same, and a quick glance down at her clothes confirmed her suspicions.

Cautiously they approached the West Gate, and were relieved to see that it was being guarded by their own soldiers. They couldn't see any evidence of fighting. The attack must have been concentrated on the east side of the town, thought Liselle.

As they neared the gate, a figure rushed from the guardroom; it was Colonel Potts. Revived by the sight of the old man, Mrs Potts ran forward and embraced her husband. The colonel hugged her back then clasped an arm around Liselle.

"I'm so glad to see you're both safe. After I had given orders to the men, I took a horse and came here as fast as I could. When I found that you hadn't arrived yet," the colonel broke off, emotion preventing him from finishing.

"We're safe now, that's all that matters," said Mrs Potts, prompting another bout of severe coughing.

"Come on, let's get you both inside," the colonel said, guiding them to the guardroom. He seated them at a small table in the single room that served as the guardroom for the West Gate.

"It's not much," he explained, somewhat apologetically, "but it has good thick walls, and one man can defend the entrance quite easily." Colonel Potts rapped the wall with his knuckles, and pointed towards the narrow door.

Liselle shivered although she was not cold. She looked around the little room. There was a single sink and on a small stove in the corner, a kettle boiled away merrily, oblivious of the conflict in the outside world.

A soldier entered and saluted Colonel Potts, who returned the salute and moved aside to allow the soldier access to the stove. He removed the kettle from the heat and soon produced mugs of tea for Liselle and Mrs Pots.

They thanked him gratefully as he set their drinks on the table in front of them. The soldier nodded courteously, and then returned outside to stand guard.

"Colonel?" said Liselle, quietly.

"Yes my dear," answered Colonel Potts tenderly. "Oh, but of course, you'll be wanting to know about your Charlie."

Liselle nodded appreciatively.

"I left him with one of our young lieutenants. I think you know him; he's the man who gave you a ride here. They were putting together a counter-attack, hoping to take back the East Gate. I left them to it, as I wanted to check on the West Gate and it gave me an excuse to see that you two were safe. They're both very bright young men, and I trust them completely. They won't do anything silly," he said encouragingly, seeing the uncertain looks on the faces of Liselle and Mrs Potts.

"However, I really must leave you now," he added sadly.

"I know," said Mrs Potts softly, rising to her feet, and once again putting her arms around her husband, "and don't you go doing anything silly either."

"I won't; I'll be back soon" he replied, then added, "and I'll bring Charlie with me."

The colonel bade them goodbye, then mounted the horse that was waiting for him outside the little guardroom. Smoke was now drifting down the street that led to the West Gate. Colonel Potts rode forward a few paces and spoke quietly to the soldier that had made the tea, and then set off quickly towards the centre of the town, disappearing into the smoke. Liselle and Mrs Potts, who had watched from the doorway, returned to their seats where they waited in silence.

They were finishing their third cup of tea when a shout from outside brought them instantly to their feet. One of the guards moved quickly to a defensive position in front of the guardroom doorway, drawing his short sword as he did so, and advising Mrs Potts and Liselle to take cover beneath the table. The little table was barely large enough to accommodate both their cups of tea, let alone provide enough cover underneath for both Liselle and the ample figure of Mrs Potts. They however, made the best of a difficult situation and squeezed in together.

From outside came the sound of running feet and clanking armour. The West Gate soldiers took up their positions. The guard at the door spoke quickly to Liselle and Mrs Potts, explaining that somehow a band of Koronians had broken through their lines and was now attacking the West Gate defences from inside the town. Liselle and Mrs Potts listened nervously, as the remaining West Gate soldiers rushed forward as one to meet the attack. There was an almighty clash of swords as the two sides came together.

Although well armed and experienced in combat, the West Gate soldiers were sufficiently outnumbered that the weight of the Koronians' attack was forcing them back towards the gate and the guardroom. The guard readied himself, preparing to lay down his life, if necessary, to protect Liselle and Mrs Potts, when suddenly there was a loud battle cry.

"It's the colonel," cried the guard excitedly.

Liselle grinned at Mrs Potts, who said, "I thought I told him not to do anything foolish."

Mrs Potts tried desperately to hide her proud smile, as they climbed out from beneath the table, and peeked around the guard. They watched Colonel Potts, still upon his horse, charge into the assailants, cutting a great swathe through their lines, throwing the Koronians into disarray. Taking full advantage of the confusion the West Gate soldiers rushed forward. They rallied round the colonel, who charged once more into the Koronians before they could regain any order. The fight had turned their way, and now it was the turn of the Koronians to fall back. Spurred on by their success, the colonel and his soldiers pressed forward their assault, driving the Koronians back up the street. It was not long before the attackers were routed and they turned and fled back into the smoky town.

Before they had time to celebrate their small victory, the soldiers, and Colonel Potts noticed three shapes, half hidden by the smoke, at the far end of the street. Three men, covered completely in bright red robes so that even their faces were hidden, were standing abreast. Calmly and motionlessly, they faced the colonel and his soldiers.

"What's going on?" Liselle asked the guard, as she frantically tried to look past him.

"They've brought mages," replied the guard grimly.

Liselle and Mrs Potts looked at one another worriedly. They knew that the soldiers would stand little chance against the fire magic of the Koronian mages. Standing immediately behind the guard, they watched as three large fireballs curved gracefully through the air before smashing down in a shower of sparks onto Colonel Potts and the advancing soldiers. The deadly orbs exploded into hundreds of smaller fireballs, inflicting lethal injuries on everyone. The colonel's horse reared in terror, pitching its rider to the floor. Colonel Potts staggered to his feet, bleeding heavily from a wound on his head, as all around him the West Gate soldiers rolled around, desperately smothering their burning clothes. Bravely, they helped one another to retreat towards their defences at the West Gate, but before they could reach safety, three more fireballs soared across the smoke thick sky. Two of the fireballs flew wide of their intended targets, falling instead onto building roofs setting them alight instantly. The third ball of flame however landed with deadly accuracy amongst the fleeing soldiers. Colonel Potts was helping a badly wounded soldier when the fireball shattered not far behind them. The force of the impact lifted them both into the air and the fire caught at their clothes. As they landed, they rolled across the ground, which extinguished the flames, but then they both lay still.

Crying out desperately, Liselle and the colonel's wife pushed past the guard and ran towards his motionless body. The guard followed them closely, unsure whether to call them back or to help. Before they could reach the stricken soldiers, another large fireball crashed into the ground in front of them, the force of it flinging them backwards. Unable to control her fall, Liselle's head hit the ground, and everything faded into darkness.

Chapter 11
Hunted

"Joe, you have to leave town, for your own safety," said his mother seriously, when she arrived home from work one day. "I'm sure I've been followed by your friend Regan. Now that the gang know where I live, they'll probably come back tomorrow when I'm at work, to see if you are here."

"I'll leave now," said Joe quickly. "I don't want to put you in any danger."

"No, wait until it's dark, then you can slip out the back way unnoticed."

Joe's mother made them dinner, giving Joe extra, for the journey ahead of him, she explained. Then she filled his pack with enough provisions for a week's worth of travelling.

"Now promise me you'll go straight to Calistan. I'll give you my sister's address. Go to her house first, and then you can search for your friends," advised Joe's mother.

"Yes, of course I will, but why don't you come with me. I don't think anybody is safe here," he replied.

Joe's mother put her arm around her son. "Don't worry about me, I'll be fine. Once you've left town, the gang won't have any reason to come near me. Anyway, the hospital needs me, and I can't leave my patients."

Joe went to bed early, hoping to get some sleep before he set off. As he lay awake, his mind turned over continually. He worried about leaving his mother, he was concerned for the safety of his friends, and the dog had wandered off two days ago, and hadn't returned. Eventually his thoughts turned to dragons and he relaxed, and gently drifted off into a dream-filled sleep.

It seemed as if he had only just closed his eyes when his mother's hushed voice and gentle touch awoke him. The house was in complete darkness, and he was glad that he had gone to bed already dressed. Quietly they made their way to the back door, where Joe had left his pack. He embraced his mother, who hugged him tightly, seemingly unwilling to let him go. Eventually she relaxed and kissed Joe gently on his forehead, before opening the door slowly.

Joe took a step out of the house into the warm summer night air. As he looked around, he suppressed a cry of alarm. Staring straight out of the darkness were two piercing eyes. Behind him, Joe's mother clamped her hands to her mouth, muffling the choking sound from her throat. Slowly, the eye's moved closer until Joe let out a soft sigh of relief as he recognised the owner. The dog sat down in front of the door waiting patiently for Joe.

Relieved, Joe's mother squeezed Joe's shoulders affectionately, and then closed the door quietly behind him. Joe walked quickly to the wooden gate at the bottom of the small garden, followed closely by the dog. He passed quickly through the gate and walked briskly down the dark alleyway that ran behind the row of small houses. Faithfully, the dog fell in beside him.

Soon they reached the edge of the town, where they cut across an open field and joined up with the road to Calistan. Several hours passed uneventfully, until slowly the dark sky grew lighter as the sun rose behind them. They paused briefly at the edge of a wood for Joe to rest and watched the sun rising over the eastern horizon.

Suddenly, the dog became very alert and his ears pricked up. He turned his head from left to right listening with one side and then the other. The dog looked up at Joe, and then trotted off rapidly along the road into the woods. Joe guessed that whatever the dog had heard could not be good, and ran to catch up.

It was not long before Joe could hear the sound of horse's hooves on the road behind them. It was still quite dark inside the woods and Joe looked around for a thicket in which to hide. Quickening their pace, Joe and the dog ran on until they reached a crossroads. Rather than crossing straight over and continuing towards Calistan, they turned left, hoping to shake off any possible pursuit.

A few yards along the road, they dived behind a low bush, and crouching down, they watched the crossroads. Almost immediately, they heard the clatter of a single horse stopping suddenly. Through the dim light, Joe could vaguely make out the rider, and was sure the man was his old adversary. Regan did not pause for long, pulling his horse round as he determined which way to go. Then he dug in his heels sharply, and continued along the road to Calistan.

Joe and the dog scrambled quickly from their hiding place and ran down the road away from the crossroads, eager to put as much distance as possible between them and Regan. Joe did not know where the road led, but it was away from Regan and that was the important thing. The road twisted and turned through the trees, making it difficult to judge the direction they were going. Eventually, the trees thinned and they emerged from the woods onto a bright rocky landscape. It stood in stark contrast to the lush green of the trees. Joe was aware that there was very little cover, should Regan or any other gang members pursue them. Deciding that the risk was greater if they returned the way that they had come, Joe and the dog followed the road onto the barren land.

The road meandered mainly southwards, curving round rocky outcrops and scrubby patches of ground covered with thorny plants. Joe stopped occasionally to listen for the sound of pursuit but heard nothing. The dog, which walked at his side, showed no signs of concern. Had Regan been following them, Joe was quite certain that his companion would hear something long before Joe did.

They did not stop for lunch, eating as they went and by mid-afternoon, they had arrived at a small dusty market town. The dog eyed the few townsfolk suspiciously, but stayed with Joe. Tired from the forced march in the morning, Joe decided to find a place to rest, intending to set off again the next morning. Joe questioned an old man sitting in front of his house, and learnt that the market was the next day, but since they had arrived early, they should have no trouble finding a room at the inn. They followed the old man's directions and found the inn without any trouble. Using some of the little money that his mother had given to him, Joe paid for one night's accommodation, much to the amusement of the burly innkeeper, whose customers were usually somewhat older than Joe was. Fortunately, the innkeeper liked dogs, so he also admitted Joe's travelling companion into the inn.

The inn was situated on one side of the market place. Their room was on the first floor and overlooked the little square. They stayed in their room for the rest of the day, and requested that their meals be brought up to them, which the innkeeper found intensely entertaining. Joe felt it prudent not to show his face too much, and after a short walk in the evening, they retired to bed early.

When Joe awoke, he could hear the bustle of stallholders setting up. The dog was standing alert and was growling at the window. Carefully Joe looked out of the window, and found himself looking down on Regan and two of his henchmen. Joe flinched away from the window, as one of the men looked up. He couldn't be sure whether the man had seen him or not, but decided not to take any chances. He dressed swiftly, grabbed his pack, and cautiously they left the room. At the bottom of the stairs, Joe glanced round the corner to look into the front room. The bar was already busy with people using the inn as a meeting place. In the middle of the room was Regan with his two friends. They appeared to be asking questions, no doubt making enquiries into the whereabouts of Joe and the dog. Ducking through a door, they found their selves in the kitchen. They startled the innkeeper, who had been working with his back to them when they entered. He spun round and took a step towards them, but relaxed when he saw who it was.

"Are you in some kind of trouble?" asked the innkeeper seriously, noticing the anxious expression on Joe's face.

"Not yet," answered Joe. "If anything, I'm trying to avoid trouble," he said holding up his hands to show he meant no harm.

The innkeeper had a kindly face, so Joe explained their predicament to him. The innkeeper listened intently, frowning as Joe explained how Culapium had been taken over by the gangs.

"We'd heard rumours about this sort of thing," said the innkeeper, nodding his head knowledgably, and rubbing his stubbly chin with one of his large hands. "Well young man, I think that you may have done this town a favour by telling me what you know. I shall pass on what you've just told me, and those rogues will soon be moved on. Now I do believe that one good turn deserves another, or so they say."

The innkeeper found an old hooded cape for Joe, and showed Joe and the dog to a back door that led out into a small alleyway. Thanking him gratefully, Joe and the dog left the innkeeper at the door.

"Here we go again," Joe mumbled to himself, as they slipped away.

They skirted the side of the inn and looked cautiously round the corner into the marketplace. There was no sign of Regan or his men, so Joe and the dog moved forward, Joe walking casually with the hood pulled down low over his face. He hoped that he would not be noticed amongst the large crowd in the market place.

"There he is, the one with the dog," yelled a familiar gruff voice.

Joe cursed himself for his own stupidity. Even if he did manage to blend in with the crowd, his companion did not. They broke into a run, weaving their way through the crowded market place. Joe could hear Regan shouting and pushing his way through the throng. Emerging at the far side of the square, Joe and the dog ran down the first street they came to. It turned sharply at the end, and chancing a quick glance behind him, Joe saw that they had not yet shaken off their pursuers. Regan and the two men Joe had seen in the inn were still following.

Too late, Joe discovered that the street they had entered had a dead end. In a frantic attempt to escape, they rushed through an open door into the nearest house. The house had just two ground floor rooms with no other exits save for a single small high window in the back room. Quickly, Joe undid the latch, threw open the window and stood back to allow the dog to leap through, which he did effortlessly.

As Joe attempted to follow the dog, he could hear their pursuers entering the house, and before he was able to wriggle through strong hands grabbed him from behind. Struggling and kicking out at his assailants, Joe looked up for the dog.

"Run," he yelled down at the dog, which was sitting waiting for Joe below the window.

The dog barked at Joe, who clung desperately to the window frame, then raced across the clear ground until it reached a rocky outcropping, where it stopped and turned round.

"Goodbye," said Joe quietly, releasing his grip on the window, and slipping back into the room. The dog barked once, as if in reply, and with a flick of his tail, he disappeared into the wasteland.

Joe faced his assailants.

"We should get a good price for you," said Regan, raising a stout club above his head.

Joe fell heavily to the floor.

Chapter 12
Thraldom

The realisation that Will was Joe's father filled Daniel with emotion. He was delighted to discover that this new friend had turned out to be the father of one of his best friends. This fact did not surprise Daniel, but he couldn't believe that he hadn't noticed the resemblance before.

"I can see it now. I don't know why I didn't realise it before. I think your eyes are the same colour," he told Will.

"So you're telling me that your friends you've talked about include my son, and he was at the orphanage with you when it burnt down?"

"Exactly that," answered Daniel, "and when I last saw Joe, he was setting out to discover what had happened to you."

They talked then, well into the night, much to the annoyance of some of the others in the hut. Daniel told Will, right from the beginning, how he and Joe had become friends soon after their arrival at the monastery. Will smiled proudly as Daniel told him of Joe's talent for Protective Charms. Will's own skills had developed rapidly under Daniel's tutorage.

"I can see where Joe's aptitude for Protective Charms came from," said Daniel.

"You're pretty good yourself," said Will.

"I guess I have improved a little, but I could never match Joe. You'll see that too when we get home."

Will smiled gently, then sighed and hung his head sadly.

"Your optimism does you credit young Daniel. I feel that I am too old to hope for much."

The next morning, Daniel and Will were crossing the quarry floor with the other slaves from their hut, when the burly guard approached them.

"Come on you, you're moving on," he said to Daniel in their own language.

The guard grabbed him roughly by his collar, and pulled him away from Will and the others.

"Wait, where are you taking him?" yelled Will.

"Somewhere you'll never get to go," sneered the guard.

"See you Will," called out Daniel frantically, as he was dragged away.

"Bye Daniel. When you see Joe, tell him I think about him every day."

The guard escorted Daniel up the ramp to the edge of the quarry. They paused briefly while the burly guard talked to another guard positioned at the top. Daniel chanced a quick glance back at the quarry, and was just in time to see the last of the slaves from his hut disappear into the mines.

They walked quickly to a small camp not far from the quarry, where they waited outside a small building. The guard huffed and sighed, clearly agitated by having to wait. Daniel muttered the Translation Charm under his breath, in readiness for whatever was to come. The guard glared at him, then cuffed him over the head.

A soldier exited the building, grunted at them and pointed over his shoulder at the door. They took this as their invitation to enter. The guard shoved Daniel ahead of him through the door. The room was a small office, and bent over the only table was a clerk who was scribbling furiously. The burly guard coughed, but the clerk continued to ignore them. A door to one side opened, and a soldier called them in to a second office. Immediately Daniel recognised him as the kind soldier that delivered him to the quarry. The soldier spoke briefly to the burly guard, who left quickly, eager to be relieved of his responsibility.

With the guard gone, the soldier turned his attention to Daniel and smiled.

"Nod if you can understand me," he said, closing the door carefully behind the guard.

Daniel nodded enthusiastically, relieved to see a familiar face. The kind soldier reached behind Daniel's neck and unclasped the slave collar.

"I don't think you need this any more," he said throwing it into a corner of the room.

"I applied for you to be transferred as soon as we had dropped you off. I'm sorry it's taken so long," he explained.

Daniel shook his head, and nodded, then shrugged his shoulders. The soldier did not understand his language, so there was little he could say.

The soldier examined Daniel closely.

"You look quite well, considering," he trailed off, gesturing in the direction of the quarry. "More magic, I suppose."

Daniel nodded his head suspiciously.

"It's alright," said the soldier. "It doesn't worry me."

Daniel relaxed again, and the soldier went on.

"You're being transferred to Thraldom. It's our capital city and most young captives go there to work in the kitchens. Several weeks ago, I had to escort a large group of them. I don't know where they came from; nobody would tell me. A raiding party brought them in from the north. I suppose you'll be joining them. In fact, I was on my way back from Thraldom, when we picked you up the first time."

Daniel looked anxiously at the kind soldier.

"Don't worry," said the soldier, seeing the look on Daniel's face. "The kitchens are a much better place to be than the mines. If it were up to me, I would send you straight home. Capturing enemy soldiers is one thing, but kidnapping children is not on. Not that I agree with using soldiers as slaves to work the mines either.

"I won't be going with you. A couple of our soldiers are due some leave, so they're going home to Thraldom. They're good men, and you'll be well treated."

The kind soldier took Daniel outside where they found two soldiers waiting. Eager to return to their families, the soldiers and Daniel left immediately. Daniel only just managed a smile and nod of gratitude for the kind soldier, who had saved him from the slave mines.

They had not gone far when one of the soldiers talked to Daniel.

"Is it true that you can understand us?" he asked.

Daniel had kept the Translation Charm going, as he wanted to know what his new escorts were like. He looked at the soldier and nodded slightly.

"Mighty impressive for one so young," said the other soldier.

"I have a son and a daughter who are both about your age," said the first soldier. "I'm looking forward to seeing them again in a few days. I'll tell them of your magic abilities, and then they might try a bit harder at school with their own lessons."

They fell silent, and walking abreast, they followed the road as it meandered through the forest.

Over the next two days, Daniel came to like the forest. He had not been able to appreciate it much when he had passed through on his way to the mines. The two soldiers treated him well, and although the pace was swift, they did not push too hard. On the way to the mines, Daniel had been fearful of his fate, but this time he knew where he was going. The kind soldier had talked about children being brought from the north and sent on to Thraldom. Daniel was sure that they must be the other orphans from the monastery. If the people who had attacked the monastery had escaped through the mountains then they would have entered Koronia from the north.

The route they followed never really left the forest. Occasionally they passed through settlements that used large clearings for farmland. Increasingly, they encountered parties of soldiers also heading south. Sometimes, they crossed checkpoints that were no more than a small hut and some form of barrier across the road. Where normally the two soldiers were relaxed and talkative to one another and to Daniel, they would straighten up and march towards the checkpoints. They showed their papers and the transfer documents that the kind soldier had provided them with, and always were soon on their way again.

On the evening of the third day of travelling, they emerged from the forest to look out on a desolate landscape. Rising out of the barren land was an enormous rock, covered with many buildings and surrounded by a large stone wall. Beyond the city, mountains towered menacingly over the land.

"Welcome to Thraldom," said one of the soldiers proudly.

He laughed when he saw the look of disgust on Daniel's face.

"It's very deceptive," explained the second soldier. "Inside the walls are many springs, and the city is full of beautiful gardens and parks. Unfortunately, you won't be seeing them today. We have to drop you off at the prison," he explained sadly.

The soldier's revelation startled Daniel; they had not mentioned it before.

"We didn't tell you because we didn't want you to worry needlessly. I'm sure it will only be temporary, before they move you on to one of the work compounds. It's not far to the prison, so we should say good bye properly now."

The soldier pointed towards a grey building at the edge of the forest, which Daniel had not noticed before.

Both soldiers patted Daniel on the back, and shook his hand. They tried to offer him advice, but Daniel struggled to understand them as his concentration waned. The sight of the prison filled him with fear and loneliness. He was going to miss his escorts.

They approached the prison in the same manner as they had the checkpoints, with Daniel between them. All of the windows had bars and there was only one entry point. The exchange was swift, once the soldiers had produced the transfer documents, and Daniel entered the prison.

An ugly guard slammed shut the solid wooden door behind the soldiers. Daniel imagined them joining their families later that night. The guard seemed to read Daniel's mind and spoke to him in his language.

"Maybe if you're lucky, they'll send you back to your family," grunted the guard.

"I lost my parents when I was young," said Daniel miserably.

"Well, that was pretty careless of you," responded the guard maliciously.

The ugly guard dragged Daniel along dark corridors, past numerous cells containing whom, Daniel knew not. Eventually, they halted outside one of the cells. The guard took out a key and unlocked the door.

"In you go," he grunted, shoving Daniel forwards into the dark cell.

Daniel tripped and stumbled forward onto his knees, wincing as they struck the hard floor. Two sinister shapes loomed over him, and Daniel choked back his fear as their pale hands reached out towards him. He recoiled from their cold touch, scurrying back against the door where he cowered, covering his face with his hands.

"Daniel, it's alright, it's us," said a familiar voice reassuringly.

Slowly Daniel lowered his hands and looked up. By the light passing through the barred window in the door, he could see the silhouettes of two figures. He leaned forward and saw that standing in front of him were the smiling faces of Joe and Liselle.

Chapter 13
Reunion

Daniel was pulled to his feet, and they were all talking at once and patting one another on the back. Then Daniel jumped as a third figure emerged from the shadows.

"Oh, this is Braun," said Joe, introducing the old man that stepped into the dim light. "He was already here when we arrived."

"How long have you all been here?" Daniel asked Joe.

"We only arrived this morning, but Braun has been here for years," answered Liselle.

"I used to be a professor at the university in Calistan. I would be still if I hadn't been captured."

"How did you end up here?" asked Daniel.

"It was silly really. I should know better at my age, but I tried to take a short cut across country. I took a wrong turn in the dark and found myself completely lost. I know how to use the stars to navigate, but they're a little difficult to follow when it's cloudy. The next thing I was in enemy territory; at least I think I was. Wherever I was, a bunch of mean looking men appeared out of nowhere, and decided that it would be better for me to accompany them. They didn't speak our language, but the sharp sword they poked me with explained everything quite clearly.

"That was over four years ago, and I've been in this prison ever since. I don't think they really knew what to do with me."

"That all sounds very familiar," said Daniel sourly, remembering his capture due to his own foolishness.

They sat down in a circle, grinning at one another in the dim light.

"Oh yes, that reminds me Joe, I nearly forgot," apologised Daniel. "I met your Father."

Joe stared at Daniel, open-mouthed. "You wouldn't lie to me about something like this, would you?" he said cautiously.

"Never," replied Daniel sincerely. "I really met your father," he said smiling.

"What's he like?" asked Joe.

"He's really nice, we became good friends. In fact I'd known him for over a week before I found out who he was."

"Go on."

"He's quite like you really. I suppose that was why we got on so well. As soon as I told him that I knew you, and had met your Mother, he wanted to know everything about you. He was very proud when I told him about how good you are with Protective Charms. He's pretty good at it himself. I can see where you get your talent."

Joe listened to Daniel in amazement as his friend described to him the father that he barely knew. He watched Daniel's lips as he spoke, leaning on his every word, lost in his friend's tale as if it were a dream.

In a round about way, Daniel told them all that had passed since their parting a couple of weeks earlier. When he had finished Liselle and Braun sat in silence looking at Joe, unwilling to speak until Joe had responded. Joe also sat quietly for some time until finally he took Daniel's hand and squeezed it firmly.

"Thank you Daniel," he said softly.

Daniel smiled gently at his friend, and then said, "What about you? How did you two end up here? Liselle, did you find your brother?"

As Liselle recanted her own tale, Joe who was already familiar with the story, sat with a wide grin on his face, recalling Daniel's words about his father.

Then it was Joe's turn to tell Daniel about his own adventures, and Daniel listened intently, amazed that they should all have been through so much, in such a relatively short time. When Joe's narration ended, they sat quietly, their minds filled with images.

Suddenly, Braun grabbed at Joe's wrist, and then he did the same to Liselle. Joe pulled away, and Braun gripped Daniel's arm and pulled back his sleeve.

"Dragon bracelets!" he exclaimed. "I don't believe what I'm seeing!" the old man said in a whisper.

The friends looked at one another with concern, covering their treasured possessions.

"How do you know what they are?" asked Liselle suspiciously.

"I saw a picture of one once, a long time ago," answered Braun, shaking his head in amazement.

"And what do you know about dragons?" asked Daniel.

"Not that much really, only what I've read in old books. They live far from our lands and never let anyone near them. There have been stories in the past of people who aided the dragons and were rewarded with Dragon Bracelets like yours. The dragons have a strange ancient magic of their own and they're also rumoured to be able to change shape but I think that's probably just a myth."

The old man stared at the bracelets in awe. Liselle put her arm behind her back. Braun jerked his head up to look at Liselle.

"Oh, it's alright. I don't want your prize. Whatever you did, I'm sure you earned your rewards justly. I doubt very much if I could remove them even if I wanted to."

He smiled kindly at them.

"In fact, you may well be wearing our ticket out of here, at least for the three of you anyway," he added mysteriously.

They watched the old man, waiting for him to continue.

"Do you know how to use them?" he asked quietly.

"What do you mean, use them?" said Joe.

"I thought not," said the old man, rubbing his chin thoughtfully. The friends looked at one another, unsure of what the old man would say next.

"You said there may be a way out," ventured Joe.

"Yes, yes of course. Now then, let me think," he mumbled, looking down into his lap and tapping his forehead with one finger.

"Well like I said, I only know what I've read in books," he said hesitantly.

"Which seems to be quite a lot so far," added Daniel, encouragingly.

Boosted by Daniel's persuasive words, the old man continued.

"This is an ancient magic, and most of what I've read is theory. After all, no one in my lifetime has even seen a dragon, let alone," he paused, unsure of what to say then continued, "well, do whatever it is that you did."

"We helped them," said Daniel softly.

The old professor nodded understandingly. "Of course, of course. Maybe one day when this is all over, and we're back in the safety of our own homes, you'll pay an old man a visit, and tell him your story."

"You can count on it," said Daniel, looking at his friends, who agreed readily.

"It's all to do with telepathy, you see," said Braun all of a sudden.

"How is that possible?" asked Joe.

"Because the dragons are telepathic," said Daniel. "But we're not, which is why we need the magic bracelets."

The others stared at him in bewilderment.

"That's right," said Braun. "The dragons can understand every thought that you have, even though you don't talk the same language. It should also work both ways, to varying degrees. But how did you know?" he said looking at Daniel.

"I think I've always known. Since we met the dragons, I mean. When the red dragon first approached Liselle, somehow I knew it would be all right. I sensed a feeling of calm coming from the dragons, which relaxed me. I felt instinctively that they meant us no harm and we could trust them. That's why I wasn't afraid. Then when they gave us the bracelets, I felt their minds inside my own. It was overwhelming, their thoughts were so intense and their memories so vast. They're old, really old. Moreover, there are hundreds of them, and they live on the other side of the world."

"Why didn't you mention any of this before Daniel?" demanded Liselle.

"Yes, I thought we shared everything," added Joe accusingly.

"I know, I'm sorry, I wanted to tell you both, honestly I did. It's so difficult to explain," he said looking down at his feet.

"Well, we'll never be able to trust you again, will we?" said Joe.

Daniel looked up quickly and was about to deny the accusation when he saw the smile on his friend's face and knew that he was teasing. Daniel grinned back, relieved that everything was still all right between them.

"I've been sharing their thoughts every night for the last two weeks," added Daniel quietly, his mind recalling some of his dreams.

Liselle and Joe looked at each other sheepishly. "Do you mean to say that we weren't dreaming?" asked Liselle slowly. "All those images were really dragon thoughts."

"So you've been experiencing the same thing?" said Daniel gladly.

They all fell silent and Braun watched while a gentle calm fell over the prison cell as Daniel, Liselle, and Joe lost themselves in their own memories. He watched their faces glow with excitement as the realisation of their connection with the dragons became clear.

"So what do we do?" Joe asked Braun, eventually breaking the peace and startling the others.

"Ah well," said Braun, "you need to concentrate hard, as if you were doing Protective Charms. Are you any good at Charms?" he asked, looking at Joe.

"I'm not bad," answered Joe, modestly.

"Good, then you shouldn't find it too difficult. Now, reach out with your minds, as though you were talking to them aloud, but do it in your heads instead."

"This is silly," said Joe, but Daniel and Liselle had both closed their eyes, and he could see from their furrowed brows that they were focusing deeply.

Joe followed suit and closed his eyes. He relaxed his mind and let his thoughts wander. Then he started to picture the gold dragon and he imagined calling out to it. Like a dog he thought, and smiled, remembering his recent canine companion, who was now lost to him.

"Well, I reckon that was a complete waste of time," he muttered after a short while.

"I don't know," said Liselle. "I thought I felt a kind of connection, as though someone or maybe something was listening."

"I felt the same," agreed Daniel. "How do we know if it worked?" he asked the old man.

"We know already," said Braun, "pull up your sleeves, all of you."

They looked at their arms and beneath their clothes they could see a soft glow. They all pulled back their sleeves, to reveal their bracelets radiating gold, red, and green as the scale effect flickered into life. They cried out with delight at the transformation. Braun gasped in awe and the friends beamed proudly.

"Quick, cover them up. Someone's coming," said Daniel suddenly.

They fumbled quickly to conceal the light shining from their wrists.

"What's all the noise, and where'd you get that light from?" growled the guard through the window in the door.

Nobody answered him and after a short while, he grunted and slumped off. They listened as his clumsy footfall faded down the corridor.

Braun whispered quietly. "It should go further, if what I've read is true. You ought to be able to communicate with one another."

They stared at Braun blankly.

"What do we do now?" asked Joe, looking somewhat bored and slightly dispirited.

"We wait," said Braun, leaning back against the cold cell wall and making himself as comfortable as possible. "I realise that is something difficult for you youngsters, but then, what else are you going to do?"

"It's a beautiful evening, perhaps we could go for a walk," suggested Liselle sarcastically, looking round at the four walls.

"How much more do you know about dragons Braun?" asked Daniel.

"More than most I suppose," he answered truthfully. "The old section of the university library is filled with thick tomes, mostly theory of course, although some of the oldest books profess to be based on fact. That's where I saw drawings of your dragon bracelets, so now you know how I came to recognise them for what they were.

"If the books are to be believed, then the last real sightings were about a hundred and fifty years ago. That coincides with the outbreak of the war, when east and west split. Of course, we've been fighting ever since and I can't help but wonder if that's not a coincidence. Before the war, men and dragons worked together and all was peaceful. Each dragon would choose a man, or a woman," he added smiling at Liselle, "to ride with them. The minds of the dragon and the rider would meld. They became almost one entity. The thoughts of one would become the thoughts of the other, and they would think as one. The riders wore magnificent armour that blended seamlessly with the dragon, and they ruled the skies, and so ruled the earth as well."

"Why did it all go wrong then? Why did the dragons leave?" asked Joe.

"That's where history gets a little sketchy. I've had to piece together a lot from only a few fragments left over from that time. I believe, and there are plenty that dispute this, that some men, we can only guess whom, grew jealous of the dragons and their riders, and turned against them. Whatever it was that happened has been covered up; there are very few records from that particular period. Whether or not any blood was spilt I do not know, but the dragons grew despondent of mankind's wrangling, and decided to leave. One day the world was filled with dragons and the next they were gone; never to be seen again," he said sadly, then added, "that is until you three came along."

They all fell quiet again, imagining a world of dragons, until Daniel broke the silence.

"I think I can feel something," he said.

"You probably have cramp," Liselle chuckled, "these floors aren't very comfortable. Tomorrow, I'm going to request a better room."

"That's a good idea," chipped in Joe, "one with a sea view would be lovely."

Braun laughed, but Daniel's face was serious, as though concentrating. He closed his eyes and the others fell silent, waiting for him to speak again. It was Joe however, who was the first to break the silence.

"You're right Daniel," he whispered, "something's coming."

Chapter 14
Dragons' Return

A large opening appeared in the prison roof as powerful talons ripped it apart. Debris from the ceiling fell on the four prisoners and they dodged the larger pieces. Through the gaping hole, they could see the starry night sky. A piercing cry cut through the stillness of the night and a large ball of green flames lit up the dark cell. The green dragon appeared over the prison.

Helping one other up, the three friends hauled themselves through the gap and up onto the roof. The dragon hovered immediately above them, his great wings beating steadily. When he saw Daniel, he tipped back his head and let out another great screech. The sound was filled with joy at being reunited with Daniel and sadness at discovering him imprisoned. The green dragon landed beside the prison and lowered his head so that it was level with Daniel. Daniel reached out and stroked the green dragon's cheek tenderly.

They slid down the roof and dropped to the floor. Out of nowhere, another dragon appeared silently, gently touching down next to Liselle. She ran to the red dragon and threw her arms around its thick neck.

From within the prison they could hear a great commotion, as prisoners and guards alike awakened to the dragon's cries. Daniel led the way round the outside of the prison to the front door that he had passed through only a few hours earlier. The green and red dragons lumbered ungainly behind them, their long tails swishing from side to side.

The door was wide open. The guards had fled in terror when they saw the dragons. Daniel and Liselle entered the prison and unlocked the cells, releasing the other captives. Set free, the prisoners could only stand and stare in terror at the huge dragons sitting contentedly outside the prison.

Joe remained outside, scouring the dark sky for any sign of the gold dragon. The red dragon nudged Joe gently, as if it understood his sadness. There was no sign of his dragon anywhere.

Braun was the last to exit the prison, and he stood with the other freed prisoners, gazing up at their unusual liberators. He turned to Daniel, Liselle, and Joe.

"What happens now?" he asked them. "It's a long way home, and I doubt whether your friends here can carry all of us."

"I wonder if they would be willing to help. Daniel, do you know?" asked Liselle.

"Yes, they want to help. Look what they're carrying," replied Daniel.

Both dragons were clutching a suit of armour in their deadly claws. The suits were the same colours as the dragons.

"But they're far too big," exclaimed Liselle taking a helmet from the red dragon and placing it on her head.

"One size fits all I expect," said Joe waving his bracelet around.

"Well done Joe, you're learning quickly," said Braun, approaching the dragons hesitantly. He reached out his hand and touched the green dragon on the side of its head. "I never expected, in all my life," he murmured.

Liselle let out a small shriek of excitement.

"It's shrinking," she exclaimed gleefully.

"You'd better hope that it stops at some point," teased Daniel.

"It's a perfect fit, and it's so light," said Liselle.

Daniel and Liselle clambered into the large pieces of armour, which shrunk immediately to fit them both, as if the suits were tailor-made.

The armour glistened and swirled like the scales of the dragons. Daniel and Liselle climbed effortlessly onto the dragons' backs, where their armour blended seamlessly with the colours of the dragons. Joe watched jealously, finding it difficult to tell where rider ended and dragon began. The dragons and their riders appeared to merge into a single entity. Their greater understanding of the dragons and the power of the bracelets united Daniel and Liselle's thoughts with those of the red and green dragons. Like the suits, the minds of both dragon and rider combined almost as one.

"So, where's my dragon then," moaned Joe dejectedly.

A sudden familiar bark from the trees caused Joe to spin round abruptly. Bounding across the ground towards him was the dog that had been his companion for the last few weeks. It leapt playfully up at Joe and ran in circles chasing his tail in delight.

"How did he get here?" asked Liselle.

"Who cares?" said Joe, dropping to his knees and burying his head in the dog's fur.

"I knew you liked me," cried Joe joyfully, as he patted the dog and stroked its head. "Thought you'd lost me, didn't you? Appreciate me now, do you? You're not quite a dragon, but I suppose you'll do."

"I wonder how he did get here," pondered Daniel.

"Maybe he's a magic dog," suggested Liselle. "Or maybe he just has a good sense of smell. Not that a dog should have too much trouble following Joe's scent."

"I heard that," said Joe accusingly, without looking up from the dog.

"I'm only saying that you have a very distinct aroma," said Liselle playfully, "nobody's accusing you of anything."

Joe grunted and Liselle grinned across at Daniel.

"Thank you," said Braun quietly, turning away from the green dragon that he had been studying to face Joe and the others. "You have made an old man very happy." Tears welled in his eyes. "After four years of imprisonment the last thing that I expected was to be set free by real live dragons; and it's all thanks to you three. It has been a privilege to meet you. Wherever you decide to go, travel safely and good luck."

He turned to Joe and said, "I hope you find your dragon. I would have loved to have seen it."

"I'll tell you what then," said Joe. "If I find the gold dragon, I'll find you and give you a ride. How does that sound?"

Braun answered quietly, "That sounds just fine, thank you Joe. I shall look out for you."

"Why do you think we're splitting up?" Daniel asked Braun.

"Why, what do you have in mind?" answered the old man.

"I think it's time we completed what I set out to do in the first place," said Daniel.

The others looked at him questioningly.

"The orphans from the monastery! I still want to find out what has happened to them," explained Daniel. "Only, I have a feeling that we may find a few more than I originally expected."

Some of the other freed men, most of who were from the West, approached the group cautiously. One of them stepped forward to speak. He explained how he had been captured attempting to rescue his kidnapped daughter, who was working in the city kitchens. He had discovered that the children were housed at night in a secure compound on the far side of the city. The ground around the compound was rocky and broken. Great fissures, impossible to cross, prevented anyone from approaching by any other route than the main entrance. The man told them that a drawbridge protected even this, completely closing off the compound.

After a brief discussion, they conceived a plan. Joe, Braun and the rest of the freed men would enter the forest, and then travel southwards. Skirting Thraldom, they would make their way towards the compound. Daniel and Liselle would fly above them, on the look out for Koronian patrols. Under the cover of darkness, the dragons should be difficult to spot. They decided that, despite its defences, access to the compound should not prove to be too much of a problem for the dragons.

With the plan agreed, and mounting concern that the guards would return quickly from the city with reinforcements, they set off. The dragons' powerful legs launched them and their riders into the air, and their great wings propelled them up into the night sky. Sharing the dragon's night vision, Daniel and Liselle were able to see Joe and the dog leading Braun and the others into the forest.

As Joe walked through the trees, the dog stuck so close to him that his head kept butting against Joe's leg. Joe smiled contentedly in the dark, happy that his companion had returned.

Chapter 15
The Rescue

They stopped at the edge of the trees to look at the compound. A great chasm lay between them and a large pair of open gates. Over the chasm, a drawbridge remained down, so gaining entry should be easy. Two burning torches on the gates lit up several guards who stood chatting idly on the far side of the drawbridge.

Flying high above the forest, Daniel and Liselle soared round in circles, alert to any possibility of attack on the group of intrepid rescuers hidden in the trees below them. Suddenly the gold dragon let out a quiet hiss. From the direction of the city, a horse was galloping towards the compound, its rider clearly intent on raising the alarm. Despite the dragons' keen eyesight, somehow the solitary horse and rider had avoided detection and were dangerously close to reaching the drawbridge.

Through the power of his dragon bracelet, Joe sensed the concern from his friends and the dragons. Even the dog became attentive, his head turning about, and his bright eyes penetrating the darkness.

Breaking from the protection of the night sky, the green and red dragons dropped silently towards the rider. Joe and the dog bolted from the cover of the trees, followed closely by their companions. The horse and rider though were already too far ahead. They raced along the side of the deep ravine, and would soon be at the drawbridge. Daniel willed the green dragon forward, hoping to cut off the messenger before he could cross the bridge. Joe and the dog soon outpaced the others, and aimed straight for the near end of the bridge.

However, all their efforts were in vain. The rider pulled his horse round sharply to cross the drawbridge. As the horse's hooves clattered noisily on the wooden bridge, the rider called out to the guards on the other side.

Daniel and the green dragon were closest to the messenger, but had to turn sharply to avoid crashing into the drawbridge. They used the depth of the chasm to pull out of their steep dive and rose again to see what had become of the horse and rider. Safely inside the compound, the messenger dismounted, and yelled instructions to the terrified guards, who were cowering at the sight of the dragons.

Slowly, the drawbridge began to rise. The rescuers had hoped to free the children with a minimum of fuss, much like their own prison break. As the dragons hovered over the deep ravine, Joe and the dog raced towards the rising drawbridge.

"No," yelled Joe, as the dog leapt forward. He grabbed hopelessly for the dog but was far too slow. The dog streaked towards the chasm, with Joe in close pursuit. The drawbridge was already half raised when the dog arrived at the edge of the ravine. It was an impossible jump, and Joe could only stand and watch in vain, as the futile attempt ended in disaster. The dog scarcely reached half way across the gap before he started dropping, and plummeted into the abyss below. Joe sank to his knees on the edge, tears welling in his eyes, watching his friend falling away below him.

As the dog fell, something strange occurred. His body shimmered and blurred, his size increased rapidly and at the same time, the dog's shape transformed into that of an immense beast. His neck and tail stretched out, and his back sprouted great leathery wings. Finally, his colour changed to a bright gold. Then, rising majestically from the deep ravine, the gold dragon flapped his immense wings to hover beside the green and red dragons.

Joe remained on his knees, looking up at the wonderful sight before him, while behind him Braun and the others gasped in amazement.

The gold dragon glanced briefly at Joe, and then landed next to the raised drawbridge on the other side of the chasm. With a single swipe of its razor sharp claws, he sliced through the ropes that held up the bridge. The ground shook with the impact of the bridge crashing to the ground. Joe, who had managed to jump out of the way only just in time, was sure that the drawbridge would smash to pieces, but it remained firm. He and the others rushed across the lowered bridge, and entered the compound.

Filled with terror, the compound guards dropped their weapons. Rooted to the spot, they gaped at the three magnificent dragons that circled slowly above the compound.

Braun and the other rescuers found the captured children quickly and released them without any hindrance from the guards, as they had hoped and planned. Some of the children saw their own fathers amongst the rescuers, and rushed to them. The orphans from the monastery recognised Joe and bombarded him with questions about the rescue and the dragons soaring overhead.

The rescuers imprisoned the compound guards in the rooms that had served as cells for the children. They met with very little resistance from the guards, some even appearing to be grateful to be out of sight of the dragons. The rescuers relieved the guards of their weapons, so that every man was armed. There was still a long way to get home, and they were bound to encounter Koronian patrols. They crossed over the drawbridge, and the dragons landed on the ground next to the now large group of men and children. The rescued children were mostly unafraid of the dragons, accepting them readily as their liberators.

Joe approached the gold dragon, which had been watching him intently. The dragon lowered his head level with Joe, and they gazed at one another, their minds already beginning to merge. Daniel, Liselle, Braun, and the others watched in silence. The dragon opened a clenched foot to reveal a golden suit of armour. Joe slipped into the armour, and instantly, it shrunk to fit him perfectly. He picked up the golden helmet and placed it over his head. Then the dragon extended his foot, and raised Joe into position on his back.

The gold dragon puffed himself up, crouched slightly, and with a roar of victory, launched into the early morning sky. The watching crowd cheered their approval, even though they were mostly unaware of the significance of the reunion between Joe and his dragon.

Daniel and Liselle darted smiles at one another, then they too followed Joe and the gold dragon into the orange sky. As their minds melded more and more with those of the dragons, they could feel the dragons' emotions, their excitement, and their love of flying. The link between Daniel, Liselle, and Joe was now so strong that communication between them required no more than a simple thought.

On the ground, Braun and the freed men encircled the rescued children and, with the sun rising steadily behind them, they moved swiftly into the trees. Overhead the ever-watchful dragons and their riders studied the forest for Koronian activity.

Joe and the gold dragon flew on ahead, searching for signs of possible ambush. Liselle and the red dragon hung back, on the lookout for pursuit. Daniel and the green dragon circled slowly above the band of men and children as they continued their escape west through the Koronian forest.

Several times, small squads of well-camouflaged Koronians attacked the group. The skirmishes did not last long; the sight of the green dragon dropping out of the sky, and blasting green fireballs into the attacking soldiers ensured swift victories.

After a brief rest at midday to eat the few provisions that they had brought from the compound, they changed direction and headed northwards for a short distance before heading west again. Joe had observed a large gathering of Koronian soldiers that lay right in their path. He relayed the information to Daniel, closing his eyes briefly to concentrate on his message. Daniel, who had landed in the small clearing where they rested, had passed on the news of the danger that lay ahead.

In this way, they reached the edge of the forest with very few casualties, and joyfully, the freed men and children walked due west towards the border. As evening approached, they arrived at one of the many forts that ran along the edge of the land. While still some distance from the fort, Daniel, Liselle, and Joe landed next to the tired but happy band of men and children. They had no desire to turn up unexpectedly at the fort and frighten their own people needlessly.

They slid from the backs of the dragons, where the jubilant party surrounded them, shaking their hands and hugging them. Some even ventured to stroke the dragons.

Eventually, they said their goodbyes, and Daniel, Liselle, and Joe watched as the people they had set free walked towards the fort. Braun was the last to leave, and grasped each of them fiercely, unable to speak.

"So what do we do now?" asked Liselle, after the old man had gone.

"Simple," answered Daniel, climbing onto the back of the green dragon. "I think that it's time for a reunion," he said looking at Joe.

Joe grinned back at Daniel, as he and Liselle took up their places on the gold and red dragons.

The dragons crouched low, and then jumped simultaneously into the air, their huge wings beating strongly. They spiralled upwards, and then Daniel, Liselle, and Joe willed their dragons northeast towards the Slave Mines of Koronia.

Chapter 16
Return to the Slave Mines

The dragons flew steadily through the morning, crossing the plains and then passing over great swathes of forest. Their riders, who had not slept for two days, dozed peacefully, safe in the knowledge that the dragons would not let them fall.

As midday approached, the dragons dropped towards the quarry, causing Daniel and the others to awaken. Below him, Daniel could see clearly the slave huts and the mine entrances, which he had left only a few days earlier.

Daniel guided the green dragon down onto the roof of the largest hut, where it immediately proceeded to tear chunks out of the roof with its giant claws. Terrified men fled the building, desperate to escape the monster that they thought had come to eat them. In their panic, many of them ran straight towards the red and gold dragons that had alighted on the quarry floor. Some of the guards tried vainly to attack the dragons, only to find themselves bowled over by a large leg or knocked back by the simple flick of a tail.

Having obliterated the large hut, Daniel and the green dragon turned their attention to the remaining buildings. Flames of emerald green burst from the dragon's open mouth, setting light to first one hut, and then the next. Such was the intensity of the dragon's fire breath that it was not long before the green dragon had reduced all of the buildings to smouldering heaps.

Beneath them in the mines, suspecting that something major was going on up above, the miners quickly overpowered the few guards and rushed to the surface. As they emerged into the bright sun, a group of heavily armed soldiers appeared at the top of the quarry. They ran down the steep path and charged towards the escaping slave workers, until the sight of the mighty dragons brought the unit up short. They backed off a short distance and then, following a brief discussion, one of them put down his sword and approached Daniel and the green dragon. The soldier removed his helmet and Daniel saw instantly that he was the kind soldier that had delivered him to the mines.

Daniel removed his own helmet, and smiled at the soldier that had been responsible for his transfer from the mines. The soldier recognised Daniel, and his jaw dropped in amazement. Quickly, he snapped his mouth shut, only to open it again to speak. Quickly Daniel muttered the Translation Charm.

"I knew there was more to you than meets the eye," said the soldier accusingly. "If I'd known you were going to come back here and destroy the place, I might have thought better about requesting your transfer," he said, his eyes sparkling mischievously.

Daniel slid down from the green dragon's back, landing lightly on the ground.

"I don't think so," he replied, reaching forward to shake the soldier's hand.

Liselle had been watching the mines as the last of the men ran out.

"Are there any more inside?" she asked one of them, as he passed her.

"None that matter," he replied, trembling at the sight of Liselle and the red dragon.

Liselle and Joe's dragons bent their heads down low so that they were level with the mine entrances. They took deep breaths and breathed fire of red and gold into the mines. Over and over again, they blasted the mines with their fiery breath until thick black smoke poured from the depths. The wood that supported the mineshafts was burning. The dragons and their riders moved back from the rock face and they watched as the slave mines burned. From deep within the mines, they could hear the crackle of flames and the creaking of wood. Occasionally there was the muffled sound of falling rock from far inside as the burnt wood gave way. Before long the cave entrances themselves were alight and a loud cheer went up as one of them collapsed, sending out a cloud of smoke, dust, and rubble. The remaining caves soon followed, each receiving the same tumultuous reception; the dragons had sealed the slave mines, hopefully forever.

As Daniel and the soldier watched the destruction of the mines with satisfaction, one of the newly freed slaves approached them.

"You just couldn't stay away, could you?" said the dirty-faced man.

"Hello Will, it's good to see you," said Daniel, embracing his friend warmly. "And, as you can see, I've brought a few friends to meet you."

"I can see that," said Will, looking incredulously at the dragons and their riders. "And very grateful we all are that you did Daniel."

Daniel smiled softly. "That's not quite what I meant," he said, beckoning to his friend on the gold dragon.

Joe slipped from the dragons back, and approached them, removing his helmet.

"Will, please let me introduce you to one of my best friends," said Daniel. "This is Joe, your son." Daniel stepped back a little, giving his friends room to meet with some privacy.

Immediately, the men with whom he had worked mobbed him. They pumped his hand and slapped his shoulders, crowding round him and assailing him with questions, just as the orphans had done on their release from the compound. Amongst them was the miserable man from Daniel's hut, who had eventually proved to be not so selfish. Imprisonment and working in the mines had taken their toll on him, and finding himself released affectedly him greatly, such that he wept openly.

For many, the excitement of their release was too much, and brought on the all too familiar bouts of coughing. Daniel quickly resumed his old job, using the Healing Charm to ease their suffering. Joe and Will were quick to lend a hand, eager to show one another what they could do. Liselle helped as best she could, but had not had the practise of the others or Joe's natural skill. The men accepted her help patiently, grateful for any assistance.

They found Liselle's kindly smile soothing, something that required no magic to ease their pains.

While the Healing Charm helped, the smoke from the smouldering huts did little to improve the situation. The nice Koronian soldier noticed this, and suggested to Daniel that they all leave the destroyed mines behind them. Daniel agreed readily, and soon they were all climbing the path up the side of the quarry. Some of the men found the ascent difficult, and were surprised to find assistance in the form of the guards that previously had treated them so cruelly. Clearly, the demolition of the mines and the presence of the dragons had altered their priorities.

Daniel, Liselle, and Joe offered their own shoulders for the weaker men to lean on, while the dragons took off and circled slowly above them. As they ascended the path, the nice soldier fell in beside Daniel and spoke to him.

"What do you plan to do now?" he asked.

"We need to get these people home," said Daniel, seriously.

"That's what I thought," said the soldier. "I have a feeling that our lives are about to change. The reappearance of dragons in the land can only be a good thing. I think that things may a get a bit complicated for a while, but ultimately I believe this war is ending at last.

"I want to help if I can, so I'm going to take a big risk and confide in you."

Daniel glanced at the soldier. His brow was furrowed and he appeared to be quite worried.

"There's going to be a big battle. Both armies have been massing in the South. I very much doubt that either side will win. Instead, many people will be hurt, and then each side will build up their troops again. It's happened before, and we just end up going round in a loop and start again.

"I believe though, that you and your friends may be able to use your newfound associates to influence the battle, and bring this long war to a conclusion."

"Thank you for telling me," said Daniel. "But what will we do about the men we've set free. They won't make it home by themselves."

"I know, and that's where we can help. If you promise to head south, and do your best to end this war, then I'll ensure that these men get to the border. We'll have to go slowly, but we shouldn't meet too many others on the road, as they have all gone south to join the rest of the army."

They arrived at the top of the quarry, where everyone paused for breath. Daniel trusted the soldier, and through his mental link with Liselle, he was able to confirm that their side at least, was indeed building up troops for a major attack. He agreed readily, and he and the soldier shook hands.

Calling together Joe, Liselle, Will and a few of the others, Daniel explained what was going to happen. Understandably, Joe and Will were unhappy to be parting so soon after meeting, but both understood the seriousness of the situation.

"I've only known you for a few minutes," said Will to his son, "but already, I'm as proud of you as any father could be."

As they said their goodbyes, the dragons landed in a clearing a short way from the quarry's edge. Daniel, Liselle, and Joe joined them, and in next to no time they were airborne again, flying swiftly southwards towards the inevitable battle.

Chapter 17
Brothers In Arms

Finding the battlefield was easy. Liselle had seen the maps in Colonel Potts' office, which marked where their troops were massing. They had expected the Koronian army to march out and meet this assault. A map on the colonel's wall had clearly showed the anticipated site of the battle. The dragons and their riders arrived as the sun was setting. From their vantage point high above the battlefield, they could see the entire battle raging below. Already, casualties littered the ground; the armies had been fighting for several hours.

Their own army heavily outnumbered the Koronian soldiers. The weight of the entire western army drove forward steadily. The Koronian army was fighting aggressively but they were no match for the well-armed western men. Repeatedly, their heavy cavalry smashed into the flanks of the Koronians, piercing their ranks and inflicting terrible casualties.

The Koronian mages were easy to spot, their bright red robes all the more evident in the evening light.

They conjured fireballs and lightening bolts, which they unleashed relentlessly upon the western army. Dotted amongst the western soldiers were the monks. They used their Power Bracelets to reflect the mages' attacks, often rebounding potentially lethal fireballs back into the ranks of the Koronians.

Every time a western soldier was injured one of the monks would translocate him to safety behind the army, and there be restored back to health using the Healing Charm.

Their own forces had a clear advantage and continued to drive on relentlessly. The Koronian troops retreated slowly, desperately fighting a rear guard action in their attempt to reach their land and the safety of the forest. They were taking terrible losses.

"Why don't they just turn and run," exclaimed Joe, watching the plight of the Koronian troops.

"I don't know," answered Daniel. "Surely they realise they don't stand a chance."

Liselle's eyes scanned the battlefield, looking for some explanation for the strange Koronian behaviour.

"They must have a reason," she mused.

Then, through the eyes of the red dragon, Liselle noticed movement in the forest.

"Look, in the trees," she yelled aloud to the others.

Koronian soldiers were advancing from the depths of the forest to the fringes, where they stopped and waited. The retreating Koronians were slowly drawing the western army into a large break in the trees, where the forest bound them on three sides.

"It's a trap," exclaimed Liselle. "They Koronians are sacrificing the lives of their own men in order to lure our army in to a dead end."

"But they can always retreat," pointed out Daniel. "Our horses can easily outrun anything the Koronians have got."

At that point, from the ends of the forest, fireballs flew into the air. Seeming to be wildly inaccurate, none of the fireballs fell anywhere close to the army, falling instead behind the advancing troops.

"They're rubbish shots," yelled Joe jubilantly.

"I'm not so sure," said Liselle worriedly.

The firestorm continued to rain down until it became apparent that the flames they could see were not coming just from the fireballs but from the grasslands themselves. Slowly, the wide opening between the trees filled with flames, until a wide band of fire stretched completely across the gap. Any chance of escape for the western army was effectively blocked.

"They'll be entirely cut off when the Koronians launch their ambush," said Liselle dejectedly.

"I suppose they're not such bad shots after all," added Joe miserably.

"But we have our own fire," said Daniel fiercely. He had not forgotten how the Koronians had treated him in the slave mines.

Daniel urged the green dragon forwards and into a dive. The dragon folded back its wings and they dropped towards the battlefield. Swiftly, Joe and Liselle followed and all three dragons plummeted out of the sky. Pulling up at the last moment, they swooped over the heads of the two armies, belching green, red, and gold fire all about them.

The two armies faltered, taken completely by surprise by the arrival of the dragons. They pulled back each fearing that the dragons belonged to the other side.

Liselle and the red dragon took advantage of the break in the fighting, and swooped between the armies, widening further the gap between them. As the dragon turned over the forest, arrows flew from the bows of the Koronians hidden in the trees. Many of the arrows found their mark, but they bounced harmlessly off of the thick scales and Liselle's impenetrable armour. The dragon blasted the trees below with crimson flames, and the shooting ceased instantly. Then Liselle guided the red dragon in to land in the space between the facing armies.

Joe and the gold dragon flew behind the western army, and over the burning grasslands. Gliding low, the gold dragon dropped slowly onto the flames, smothering a large patch of them with his great bulk. Frustrated shouts from the mages hidden in the forest edges heralded a barrage of new fireballs, this time aimed with perfect precision at Joe and the gold dragon. Impervious to both flames and magic, the gold dragon retaliated with brilliant fire that soon silenced the Koronian mages.

Daniel and the green dragon soared around the edge of the battlefield. Arrows, fireballs and lightening bolts from the hidden Koronians bombarded them, but to no effect. Several well-aimed blasts of green fire were all that were required to send the attackers scurrying deeper into the forest for safety.

Very quickly, all fighting came to a halt, as both sides waited to see what would happen next.

Liselle wanted to find a familiar face in the western army, so urged the red dragon closer to the front ranks. The soldiers dropped back fearfully, but stopped when Liselle removed her helmet. Their fear turned rapidly to amazement when they saw who was riding the great red dragon.

One of the soldiers immediately pushed his way forward, and carefully approached Liselle and the red dragon. As he neared, he removed his own helmet. This time, Liselle had no problems recognising her brother, and slid from the dragons back and into his warm embrace. Behind Charlie followed Colonel Potts who gave Liselle a hug that would have crushed her, but for the dragon armour.

"Liselle?" said the colonel incredulously.

"I just had to make sure that you were both alright," she said throwing her arms around the bemused Charlie and Colonel Potts.

"Perhaps you'd care to explain," said Charlie.

"About what?" asked Liselle.

"Nothing really, but maybe you could tell us about the dragons?"

"Oh those, yes I'd almost forgotten" replied Liselle playfully.

The green and gold dragons circled gracefully above the battlefield, keeping a careful eye out for anyone looking to restart the fighting. They watched as Liselle talked to Charlie and Colonel Potts. Through their psychic link, Daniel and Joe knew that Liselle was explaining how they came to arrive at the battle on the backs of three great dragons. She also told them of their intentions for putting an end to the war. After many generations of conflict, the return of the dragons gave them the opportunity to stop the fighting. The land, divided for so long, finally had a chance to reunite.

Suddenly Joe and the gold dragon saw movement at the front of the Koronian ranks, and they dropped immediately into a steep dive. Daniel and the green dragon followed them closely. A small band of soldiers was marching steadily towards Liselle, Charlie and the colonel. The dragons landed a little way in front of the advancing group, and opened their mouths menacingly. Daniel and Joe then saw that the men were unarmed and had removed their helmets to show that they meant no harm.

A group that included Liselle, Charlie, and Colonel Potts walked out to meet the Koronians. Midway between the two armies, soldiers hastily erected a large tent, where the leaders could meet and so, the peace talks began. Daniel and Joe remained outside with the dragons, their presence a stark reminder of what would happen if anyone resumed fighting. Liselle stayed in the tent so that the men inside would not forget what had brought them together.

Throughout the night, messengers ran back and forth between the tent and the waiting armies. Slowly, bit by bit, both armies broke up as the different sections received instructions to return home. Finally, after a very long night of negotiations, Liselle left the tent to be with Daniel, Joe, and the dragons. There was no need for her to explain anything. They had listened in to everything that Liselle had heard.

"Is that it then?" asked Joe.

"I think so," replied Liselle.

"Both sides have decided to stop fighting?" asked Daniel.

"It does look that way. I really think we might have peace," said Liselle through a big yawn. She stretched out her arms, and straight away, the red dragon slipped his long neck between them. Liselle hugged the great dragon tightly. As she did so, the dragon slowly pulled Liselle in close, encircling her with its long body and tail, forming a makeshift nest around her.

"Thank you, that's lovely and comfortable," she said closing her eyes, and promptly fell fast asleep.

Chapter 18
A New Beginning

Peace across the land had lasted a month without incident. Both sides had stayed true to their word, and there had not been any attacks. Many people had returned home already, eager to see what remained of the villages and towns that they had abandoned.

Daniel, Liselle, Joe, and the dragons had kept up a continuous presence in the skies, flying from west to east and back again. No one was in any doubt that once again, dragons had returned, and all saw it as a good sign.

Trading between the two sides of the country had picked up quickly, as merchants were swift to take advantage of new markets and customers. The people soon adapted to a better life, one without fear of invasion, where they could make plans for the future.

Shortly after the peace talks, Joe had led the others to Culapium, where he had an old score to settle. They landed in the garden of the mansion inhabited by Regan's gang. The dragons' fiery breath soon set the old building ablaze. Gold, red, and green flames engulfed the wooden building, rapidly razing it to the ground. The gang members fled in terror, all except Regan, who the gold dragon scooped up lightly in his jaws. They deposited Regan with Culapium's new law enforcers. Despite the nature of his capture, Regan had not been subdued completely. When he saw Joe with his helmet removed, Regan shouted at him, threatening that one day he would get Joe and his little puppy of a dog. The gold dragon quickly morphed into the dog, then blurred back into a dragon, blasting a huge ball of gold flame over the top of Regan's head. After a short spell in prison, nobody ever saw the terrified man again, although it was rumoured that he had found peace, working on a little farm near the sea in the west.

Joe kept his promise to Braun, surprising him one day in the grounds of the university in Calistan. They spent a whole day and night flying over every inch of the re-united land. The experience had a profound effect on the old man, who became the university's professor of dragon knowledge, a subject that had suddenly proved very popular.

One day, as Daniel, Liselle, and Joe returned from a visit to Thraldom, the young dragon that they had rescued appeared in the sky above them. There was a brief communication between the dragons, and then they all turned towards the village of Crickle, flying on in silence.

They noticed that a bright multi-coloured dragon had joined the young dragon, and then one by one, more and more dragons appeared from the clouds and from the skies around them. Dragons of every colour imaginable surrounded the gold, red, and green dragons and their riders, their iridescent scales glistening and shimmering in the bright sunlight.

They flew low over Crickle, where the villagers waved and cheered at the dragon riders, who had brought about an end to the war. Gliding down softly, the gold, red, and green dragons alighted gently on the lawns of the old burnt out monastery. Repairs to the building had started soon after the end of the fighting. Many people had volunteered to help with the repairs.

Charlie had been one of the first to return. He had felt a pang of sadness since hearing about the fire, and had decided that maybe life at the orphanage had not been quite so bad.

Joe's parents, re-united at last, had moved to Crickle so that Joe would be close to his friends. They too had chosen to help rebuild the monastery.

Mrs Potts decided that it was time for Colonel Potts to take life easier, so he had taken up command of the small barracks at Southersby. One of his first orders was to send soldiers to assist with the monastery, a job that he decided to oversee himself. Of course, wherever the colonel went, Mrs Potts accompanied him to ensure that he would not get into trouble.

With nowhere else to go, the monastery orphans had found temporary accommodation with the villagers of Crickle, on the understanding that they would help with the reconstruction and return to the monastery as soon as they could.

Even Brother Bartholomew had made it back. His sister had returned him to full health. The monastery was a sad place for him and the others; they all felt a great loss remembering the monks that had lost their lives defending the children.

They all stopped working on the repairs to watch as the three great dragons landed in the monastery grounds.

Daniel, Joe, and Liselle slipped gently down the sides of the green, gold, and red dragons. Their armour went loose about their bodies. Sadly, they removed the protection that had become so familiar to them, and placed it on the ground with the helmets. As their thoughts separated, returning them to their own senses, they felt an immense wrench. Joe put his arm around Liselle's shoulders as she sobbed uncontrollably. The dragons lifted up their heads and let out a heart-renting cry, as they also felt the chasm left by the parting of their minds.

The red dragon nudged Liselle gently and she threw her arms around its thick neck and squeezed tightly. The green dragon lowered his head level with Daniel, allowing him to stroke the bridge of its nose. The gold dragon shimmered briefly, and then shrunk to the familiar shape of the dog that had been Joe's companion through so much. Joe buried his head in the dog's fur one last time and patted his head fondly.

The dog slowly changed shape back into the immense form of the gold dragon, and stepped back from Joe. Slipping away from Daniel and Liselle, the red and green dragons joined him. They crouched low simultaneously, and then with a force that shook the ground, they launched themselves into the air to join the other dragons flying above.

Now hundreds of dragons filled the skies. Swooping, diving, and soaring, they resembled a huge swirling flock of birds. They flew around one another, lighting up the evening sky with their fiery breaths. Like a hypnotic dance, they whirled about in a display that was visible for miles.

Joe's parents, Charlie, Colonel and Mrs Potts, Brother Bart and the orphans joined the three friends and they watched the spectacle for hours as if held in a trance. They were unable to see their own dragons, but could still sense their presence. They could feel the minds of all the dragons, which felt as if they were on the edge of a vast deep ocean in which they dare not swim. To join wholly with so many enormous minds would be to lose completely one's own mind.

They watched though the night, the dragons belching flames into the darkness. Not until the first rays of dawn did the dragons begin to peel away, heading for their home on the other side of the world.

As the last dragon disappeared into the distance, the first rays of dawn fell on the monastery. Charlie was the first to break the silence.

"Do you think we'll ever see them again?" he asked.

Daniel, Liselle, and Joe all smiled and nodded in unison.

"How can you all be so sure?" asked Brother Bartholomew.

Laughing joyfully, they held up their arms to show everyone.

"They left us our bracelets," explained Daniel.

The little group stared in awe at the beautiful bands fixed permanently about the wrists of the three dragon riders. Whereas before, when the dragons had left them behind and the bracelets had grown dull, now they continued to shine brightly. This time the tiny shimmering scales on the dragon bracelets would not fade away but would go on gleaming forever.

Lightning Source UK Ltd.
Milton Keynes UK
20 April 2010

153096UK00001B/5/P